The Last Ride Together and Other Stories

Stories inspired by women

The Last Ride Together
and Other Stories

Roop Chand

To my girl friends

www.orientpaperbacks.com

ISBN 13: 978-81-222-0479-7
ISBN 10: 81-222-0479-1

1st Published in Orient Paperbacks 2009

The Last Ride Together and Other Stories

Cover Design by Vision Studio

Published by
Orient Paperbacks
(A division of Vision Books Pvt. Ltd.)
5A/8 Ansari Road, New Delhi-110 002

Printed in India at
Saurabh Printers Pvt. Ltd., Noida

Cover Printed at
Ravindra Printing Press, Delhi-110 006

Contents

Author's Preface

The eleven short stories included in this volume are based on the true incidents which I had been vignetting in my diary for the last fifty years in my life. Some of the short stories like 'Adhunika' are based on the incidents arising from cultural conflict in urban life in modern India. We all mask our inner naked selves under the garb of social norms — but very few have the courage to accept the fact that we live most of our life wearing a mask. Of course there are exceptions.

In the times we live in, cultural conflicts between traditional and modern way of life lead to many day-to-day dilemmas for the youngsters. I have brought out many challenging issues in these short stories for sociologists to frame new norms. Is life meaningless or meaningful? Such issues riddle the mind of modern youth.

Women are the main source of inspiration in inking these creative pieces.

Divorce

It was a hot summer day. The weather was sultry. The breakdown of electricity supply had turned the room cooler into a piece of junk. The living room had become intolerably stuffy.

Suvarna was feeling uneasy; the weather was just one of the reasons. A little while earlier she had had a row with Sudan and was feeling agitated about it. In fact she was overwhelmed with disgust and could think of no way that would solve her problems and help her restore smooth relationship with Sudan. She knew that it was futile to think of working out any adjustment with him in the existing circumstances. She was regretting getting married to him. She had even contemplated filing a case of divorce in the court of law.

She came out to the terrace. Her thoughts were focused on the unbearable pain and agony that Sudan's kicks and blows caused her, when her attention was diverted by a tiny honey sucker bird, fluttering around a clump of leaves on the mango tree in the small kitchen garden adjoining the terrace. Perhaps it was trying to find some cool place. Soon it found a shady branch and twittering happily settled on it. It happiness was however quickly shattered by a crow scooping fast towards it out of the blue sky. Calculating its chances of evading the attack, the bird quickly flew off the mango tree and sought shelter on an amaltash across the road. At that moment Suvarna envied the bird.

'Wretched creature has gone,' murmured Suvarna to herself, as she saw Sudan drive his car out and zoom away on to the road.

The crow had appeared again. Ouch! It swooped over the honey sucker bird. The tiny bird tried unsuccessfully to escape the deadly attack. It fell down injured into the garden. The bird looked frightened and was gasping for breath.

Gently Suvarna picked the bird up. Seeing it injured she put a bandage around the bleeding leg. There was fear in the eyes of the bird. Caressing and soothing the bird, she perched it on a potted plant in the lobby, leaving the door open for it to fly away.

As she stood gazing at the bird, there was a knock at the door. 'Must be Nandita,' she thought who had to come and see her. Nandita was a dear friend. But Suvarna was wrong. It was not Nandita who stood at the door, but someone she least expected. She was pleasantly surprised to see the sight of the visitor at her door.

For a moment she could not believe that Tapan stood in front of her. She almost jumped with joy. 'Tapan!' she exclaimed and rushed towards him, embracing him in her arms. For that moment she forgot all her miseries and sorrows and felt absolutely secure. A momentary glow appeared on her face. Loosening her arms, Suvarna led him inside.

'Tapan, come in, and sit down. Tell me where had you been hibernating all these long years?'

'Yes, these have been long, tough years for me, but you must have an excellent time,' he said entering the lobby. Hearing his words Suvarna felt a sharp stab of pain inside. She turned pensive once again. Heaving a sigh, she replied, 'Oh no, time had been hanging like an enormous solid rock around me.'

Tapan selected the chair next to the door opening into the terrace. Taking his seat, he looked at her face. There was no hiding the pain in the eyes and the sorrow in her tone she tried to hide. He could sense that all was not well with her.

'Are you not feeling well? You are looking pulled down,' he asked. Suvarna kept quiet. Not receiving any answer, he enquired about Sudan.

'I do not know where the hell he has gone,' she replied indifferently. 'And I couldn't care less.' There was suppressed anger and indignation in her voice.

Tapan was convinced that something had gone wrong between Sudan and her, and not everything was well, but he kept his reaction close to himself. A period of silence followed as they studied each other trying to understand the cross-currents of emotions within the other. There was no mistaking the compassion even as they tried to keep their expressions normal and not show what they felt.

The woman sitting in front of him was the not the same lively Suvarna Tapan had known three years ago. Like wise for Suvarna. Tapan was not the same humorous young man who had been full of jest and kept every one gushing with love for life. What a change! What a change had taken place in their lives in the past three years.

In spite of all her problems, Suvarna had maintained herself and was still a charming, graceful woman. Tapan on the other hand wore a long wild beard practically covering the entire face; his long hair were unkempt and fell around his shoulders. He wore a pair of rough trousers and a blue canvas jacket. Wrinkles on his face gave an impression that he had gone through hard times.

'You did not tell me, where you had been all these years?' asked Suvarna, breaking the silence. Tapan turned serious at her question. He seemed to be contemplating something deep and personal before replying to her. In a low tone he said, 'Forget about me Suvarna, I want to know how the life had been with you?' There was uncharacteristic gravitas in his voice.

'No, you tell me about yourself, please,' pleaded Suvarna.

He looked searchingly at Suvarna. Was she hiding some deep melancholia behind the make-believe smile, he wondered. 'I was travelling like a gypsy, first for sometime in India and then in Europe. I walked for months at a stretch, sleeping at the roadside or on the pavements, and sometimes in the way side inns. I was on a mission to explore a new world of love and peace. Life was hard — very hard. I often thought that my earlier life of living in an ivory tower had toppled like a like a house of cards, but still somewhere something deep inside me compelled me to live, and live on. Then I came back to India.'

Suvarna — the same Suvarna, who had fought with her parents and relatives to get married to Sudan, but was now seriously thinking of filing for divorce, was pleased to have Tapan unexpectedly visiting her at such a difficult time for her. But she was not sure how Tapan would react if she told him about her decision to separate from Sudan. The two had not even been in communication with each other for three long years. Her hesitancy was only natural. They had been cut off from each other.

Tapan's feelings were not very different. The informal friendly feelings of the old were missing. The emotions were not the same, they seemed different. He imagined that some strange complex had come between them, which made them almost like strangers. Yet he was not sure. Was his imagination playing tricks? Had his feelings changed? There was an element of doubt within him. Yet he was sure that some thing had changed in Suvarna. The old spiritual love and affection were missing. Her behaviour lacked the warmth he remembered and cherished. But it was only natural. Once she was married to Sudan, it had to happen so. Tapan had also to reconcile to the fact that she was no more his beloved.

From the corner came the twittering sound. The injured honey sucker had fallen down trying in vain to fly. Suvarna got up, picked the bird and placed it back on the plant. The injured bird also attracted Tapan's attention. 'Is it your pet?'

'No it is a free bird. It has injured its leg. I will set it free as and when the leg is healed.'

Inspite of all other changes, Suvarna still remained a compassionate and a kind person, noted Tapan. His thoughts went back to the college days when close friendship existed between them. He had been particularly attracted by her compassionate nature. She was the one who empathized and shared everyone's pain and sorrow, while others expressed sympathy and moved on. She was known for her kindness and ever willing to help friends. Their friendship had grown and the two of them, Suvarna and Tapan, had become very special for each other. Then out of the blue one day she had announced that she was going to marry Sudan. And that had been the end of their relationship. He would have avoided this visit to Suvarna today; but his mother had insisted that he go.

'Suvarna, my mother told me that you had been trying to contact me. Today she asked me to come and see you. I hope everything is fine with you.'

'Yes Tapan, it is true that I was trying to contact you desperately. I wanted to tell you something. Something important and serious. I am divorcing Sudan; and I am glad that you have come at such a crucial time.'

She felt quite relieved after speaking out her mind. The depression, she was feeling a while ago had disappeared; and a kind of glow appeared on her face.

Tapan contemplated on her words, and then spoke. 'So the mystery is over; and I can understand the cause of your mental agony. But I cannot understand why you want to take divorce. Despite your parents and relatives' strong objections to your decision to marry Sudan, it was you, only you, who had resolved to get married to him and had married him. And now you want a divorce. Why? Why? What has changed that you should seek divorce? Why this confusion?'

'I am not confused. And I do not know how explain what I have been going through these years', she said, staring at the injured bird. Tears welled up in her eyes which she tried hard to hide.

'I am sorry if I have hurt your feelings,' said Sudan looking at her aggrieved face.

'No, not in the least. You have not hurt my feelings, Tapan. I am upset at my own follies. What a life! There is no such thing as love in this world. I was foolish to marry Sudan. I loved him so much that I defied all my nearest and dearest — my parents, my friends – and married Sudan.'

'I think you confused marriage with love. Marriage is a social contract between a man and a woman,' said Tapan. 'Love is a very personal emotion. It is an expression of divine feelings. It can be a one-sided emotion or a two-sided affair. It is a state of mind that is pure and selfless in nature,' he continued, now seemingly lost in his own thoughts.

'How I hate Sudan….' There was more anguish than revulsion in her tone.

'There is a very thin line separating love and hatred. One often merges into another. Some time when you hate a person it may imply that your love has not been reciprocated to your expectations. In love and in hate there are strong emotional bondages. When both man and woman have deep spiritual vibrations and an inner urge to merge mentally into each other's consciousness, it is a state of love; but when spiritual vibrations clash and seek self identification in the beloved, it often leads to hatred,' said Tapan. 'Possibly you could not find yourself identifying with Sudan's character. I do not for a moment doubt your basic nobility, but putting it in the social context, I would say that both partners have to make adjustment in a marriage. If you can adjust with Sudan it would be good for you.'

'You advise me to make adjustments. You, who often talked of freedom — absolute freedom – with conviction a couple of years ago. I think you have changed your views about human relationships. Do you remember that besides my parents, you also discouraged me from getting into the bondage of marriage?

You talked about freedom in life and of living, and now when I want my freedom from these bonds, you advise me to adjust with a criminal.'

Suvarna was clearly agitated. She had not expected this response from Tapan. It broke her down. She got up and almost ran to her bedroom sobbing. She was hurt, very badly hurt and let down. By Tapan, of all the people.

Bewildered by her unexpected reaction, he followed her into the room. She stared at him. He looked back, confused but meeting her gaze. No words were said, but their attention was focused on each other. With deliberate movement Suvarna turned around and exposed her back to him. There was no need for her to say anything. The once smooth and flawless skin of her back was now scarred with less-than-fully-healed signs of physical blows. 'See these… Sudan beats me often and without mercy. He tortures me — both physically and mentally.'

Tapan was aghast. He had always known that Sudan was an opportunist, but even in his wildest dreams he would never have thought him to be a sadist brute. He began to understand the sheer hell Suvarna had been living through.

'I am really sorry, Suvarna. Never would I have imagined this kind of hellish life for you. All the same you must get in control of yourself. Stop crying. It will not get you anywhere. Have faith in yourself. I am with you in your fight against this injustice.' He knew his words meant little, very little, but that was all he could offer. Maybe she was better left alone. Reluctantly, he went out of the room.

He looked at the injured honey sucker, fragile, hurt and unable to fly. Very much like what Suvarna must be feeling now. It also reminded him of how helpless he had felt when he had injured his leg in an accident during his college days. Suvarna had lovingly looked after his needs and nursed him back to health...

When Suvarna came out she had freshened herself up and was more in control of her emotions. 'I wish I would have told you all about this situation earlier…' she said, looking at him. 'Just your presence is a great source of moral support. Thank you.' There was unmistakable sincerity in what she said.

'Suvarna, do not allow Sudan to exploit you and your loving nature. You can count on me for all help,' he said, looking at his watch. 'But I have to go now.'

'Where are you going?'

'Shimla,' he replied. 'I have some work there.'

'Can't you postpone your trip… for my sake?' she asked. There was affection in what she said, and the same tenderness in her eyes that he was so used to seeing in college.

'Do you really need my presence?'

'Of course, I will speak my mind to that barbarian in your presence. He will not hit me if you are around,' she said.

Tapan realized the sensitivity and urgency of the situation. Besides, deep in his heart his love for her was still alive. He still felt for her. 'All right I will stay back. Have you contacted any lawyer for divorce case?'

'Yes I have. Possibly she may come today. I telephoned her but she was not at home. I have left a message with her maid that she must come and see me. You know her... Nandita.'

'You mean Miss Patriot is your lawyer.'

'Yes your Miss Patriot is my lawyer.'

Both laughed at their description of Nandita as 'patriot'. Tapan had always called Nandita as Miss Patriot. The atmosphere had suddenly become lighter. They talked about good old days and then the reference came about Suvarna's creative pursuit.

'Tell me, how are you doing with your paintings,' asked Tapan.

'It all ended with the marriage,' replied Nandita, once again a hint of sadness creeping into her voice.

As they talked about the 'good old days' and relived their memories, the telephone rang. Thinking that Nandita might be calling her, Suvarna quickly picked up the receiver.

'Hello… Yes, this is Suvarna speaking… what… he met with an accident? Oh no…' The receiver slipped out of her hand. For a moment she stood still, and sank down into the chair.

The ceiling fan whirred to life. The electricity supply had been restored. She looked up, whether at the fan or the Almighty, even she did not know. She did not know whether she should cry or laugh.

Tapan asked her, 'Has there been an accident…?'

'Sudan,' she said gravely.

'Where, what happened? Is he alright?'

'He is dead and in a hospital. There was a call girl with him.'

She looked at the honey sucker, who was trying to fly. She got up and pushed the bird through the open door. The bird flew. Suvarna watched it fly over the mango tree and high into the sky.

Then she turned and walked back to where had been sitting, next to Tapan.

'Do your parents know about your situation?'

'I did not tell them about my life. In fact no one knows about it except the woman who used to come with Sudan dead drunk at late hours in the night...,' her voice trailed off.

Silence descended once again. Each preoccupied in personal thoughts.

Overcoming her pain and grief, Suvarna asked Tapan to help in organizing the cremation. Tapan merely nodded his consent.

After the cremation he said to Suvarna, 'Mysterious are the ways of nature.'

'Yes Tapan', she said with deep affection, 'Nature divorced us before I could.'

Ishtar's Guest for the Night

On a hot summer evening, he was the solitary traveller on this country side road leading through rocky landscape. The blazing sun had gone down in the west. Though the hot wind had calmed down, yet the atmosphere was still quite hot. He glanced now and then at the landscape just to break the monotony of the drive.

He saw an old monument spreading over thousands square meter on a rocky land. It was not very far off from the road. Next to it appeared a hamlet with evening smoke rising from its houses and spreading over the old monument. While he was glancing over there, he felt as if some one was calling him from behind. He turned his neck to look at the back but there was nothing. All of sudden the speed of the motor cycle was getting slow. Though the engine was functioning perfectly well, but the machine came to halt. He parked it off the road and inspected all over its body. 'Aha! It is nothing serious.' He uttered and found the chain had come off from the rear wheel. The chain was loose and it might have come off when he drove over a pot hole. He had been on move for the last three hours and had covered over two hundred kilometres at a stretch. So he thought to relax for some time before fixing the chain on the wheel. He stretched his limbs and sat down on a stone lying near by him. The stone was very hot, so he got up immediately and sat down on his motor bike.

He was looking at the old monument and wondering whether it was a palace or a tomb? Just then some village women descended down the hillock behind him. They were conversing softly. When they came nearer he looked at them with curiosity. He noticed a beautiful young girl who hid behind an elderly woman on getting his attention. He laughed. 'Why are you scared of me? I am not a ghost,' he said. The old woman smiled casually, and looked at him. 'Yatri?' she asked.

'Yes, I am a traveller. Is there an inn in the village to stay for the night?' he looked at the woman.

'You shall find a decent place in the village if you want to spend the night,' she said and paced briskly with other women.

He ogled at the young girl till she was out of sight. He felt as if he had lost his peace of mind. He looked at the setting sun. Thinking that soon it would be dark and difficult to set the chain, he got up and fixed the chain. Instead of continuing his journey he decided to pass the night at the village.

He drove slowly on the dusty road and reached the outskirts of the village. There near a well, an old man was sitting quietly, whom he asked if there was a place to spend the night in the village. The old man asked him, 'Are you a tourist?'

'Yes I am a tourist and want to break my journey here.'

Pointing his finger toward a verandah, the old man asked him to park his motor cycle there. The old man got up and moved towards the other side of the well, took out his rosary and sat down on the cemented platform under the branches of a bodhi tree to perform his evening prayers.

He moved his motor cycle toward the verandah and parked near a pillar. He took his bag, placed it on a bench and took out soap and a towel, for having a bath at the tank next to the community well. But he did not want to bathe at the tank without permission of the old man and he was performing his prayers. He did not want to disturb him in his prayers. While he was thinking of his problem to have bath, a young girl came with a lantern and placed it at the mantel. This was the same girl whom he saw at the road side. He was anxious to open himself to her, so he asked her if he could have a bath at the tank near the well. She was surprised to see him. She did not answer him and went back inside her house and told her mother, that the stranger they met at the road side is sitting in verandah.

Her mother came with her and asked him, 'Has the old man permitted you to stay here.'

'Yes please, he has very kindly permitted to park my motor cycle here, but I will not give you people any trouble. I will sleep on the platform next to the well. I am feeling reek, if I am allowed, I may have bath at the tank,' he said.

'Yes you may have,' the woman said. She asked her daughter to give him a bucket and a *lota*. The young girl went inside and brought a bucket and a *lota* and gave him.

'Do not pollute the water. You may have water in the bucket and wash far from the tank,' she said and went away.

The young girl went inside the house with her mother. The young tourist had a good bath and felt fresh. After the bath, he spread his sleeping bag on the cemented terrace near the well and relaxed on it. The moon had risen in the east but it was not bright as yet. The old man finished his prayers and having a glance at the young man; he went into verandah and sat down on a diwan. He called his grand daughter and told her to provide meal to the uninvited guest at the terrace.

When the young girl came with meal and gave him, 'What is that old monument known as?' he asked.

'Oh you don't know? That is Ishtar's Tomb. You should not go there after eating sweets. You will never come back. My bapu went there once after eating pudding and never returned.' She said and asked further, 'do you want anything else?'

'No, thank you,' he said.

'You did not like the food. Shall I get you some *gur*? It is good; you may like to have it,' she said. Now she was not scared of him.

'No, thank you. I do not need any thing now,' he said and got up to wash the utensils.

'No! No! You should not wash the utensils, otherwise I will suffer from sin. You are our guest and we do not allow our guests to wash utensils,' she said and picked up the utensils and saying *namaste* went away.

Though he shared a few moments with this young girl; but he felt as if he knew her for long. She left a deep impression on his mind. He did not ogle at her now. When she was striding back to her house, he looked at her with affection.

He looked towards west at the silhouette of the Ishtar's Tomb against the sky light; and thought of going there. He took his torch and moved towards the tomb. An unknown form whispered in his ears from behind. He turned his neck to look what it was, and saw a baboon sitting on the branch of a bodhi tree. His eyes were burning red. He gibbered for a while, jumped on the muddy road and disappeared in darkness. He treaded on rocky track. When he was not very far from the tomb, his torch went off. He thought that the cell might be discharged. Some how, he reached the main gate of the tomb. He sensed that some one was following him, so he looked behind and saw a dark shadow disappearing in a cluster of trees.

He entered the gate and heard a sound, 'Hush! I will blow your head.' A bat fluttered away from a hole in a cupola. A stone fell down. He heard a woman's wailing. There was commotion which stirred his mind. 'Abduction! Ishtar's abduction!'

Ha... Ha... Ha... laughter of manly sound resounded in the ruins. The cry of the woman got lost in the fleering laughter of a giant who was running with a beautiful woman on his shoulders towards a gate in north direction. A baboon ran after the giant.

Silence prevailed for some time. He walked on a terrace in an open space and looked at an old man who looked like a skeleton, lying on the floor with his head on the lap of a damsel. A lamp was burning in the back-round on a grave stone. A shadow appeared from a side vault, moved towards the old man and stood on the door. The old man opened his eyes and looked at the black shadow. 'Who are you?' the old man asked.

'I am your escort — an agent of death.'

The man looked at the pale face of the young girl. Then he turned his hollowed eyes to the black shadow.

'Can you wait for some moment?'

'Yes certainly, I will wait as there are still some moments left for you.'

'Ishtar, do not shed tears on my death,' he said and fell into eternal silence.

The lamp on the grave flickered for a second and extinguished. The young girl removed the dead body from her lap. A woman with long teeth and vulture like fingers appeared and took away the dead body of the old man in the main dome. The beautiful young girl walked up to me. 'You are the guest of Ishtar for the night.'

Ishtar! Ishtar! Ishtar! The sound resounded in the ruins for some moments and died. Huki hu… Huki hu… Huki Hu... A jackal howled in the far off field.

He did not say a word to the young girl. However she caught his hand and asked him to follow her. His legs moved automatically behind the young damsel. She moved in an aisle and then through a flight of stairs came in a well decorated chamber. Her glowing face in the bright light of a lamp gave him an impression that she might be Ishtar. She asked him to take seat on a comfortable coach. She pulled a chain and a bell rang in the side room. A giant came out with a chopper in his hand. The young man was carrying a revolver in his side pocket. When he saw the horrible looking giant, he tried to pull it for his safety in eventuality of an attack by the giant. Relax some one whispered in his ears. He turned his head to see who was whispering. He saw a snake creeping up on his coach, but as soon as he looked at it, it disappeared. The giant bowed his head before the beautiful woman and asked for her order. She asked the giant to send her maid with drinks for the guest for the night. The giant disappeared and after a while a young maid came in with a tray of drinks. The beauty of the evening asked her maid to take care of the guest for the night and walked away in another chamber. The door closed automatically behind the woman.

The maid gave him the drink. 'So you are the victim for the night. Take your drink and celebrate life till the last moments.' He could see her holding tears in her eyes. 'Take care of yourself, I am going as the beauty of the night will join you shortly,' she said and walked into the side room. He threw the drink out through a window over a plant. He thought that he had seen her some where, but he could not recollect where and when he saw her. While he was thinking about the maid, the beautiful woman came. She was smelling temptation. She was wearing pale white gown and was looking seductive.

'Have you finished your drink?' she asked. 'Yes I have,' he said. 'Then, let's move.' He was puzzled for a moment but regained his wits and asked, 'Where?'

'You do not know? Ha! Ha! Ha!' she laughed loudly and asked him to follow her.

She picked up the lamp and holding his hand moved through a door into a deserted garden. She stood under an old tree where all kind of night birds were sitting on it and were making queer noise. She moved further with him near a vaulted room. There, he saw a heap of skulls and bones. Some black giants were moving out of the clamps of the old tree. He saw some goblins pulling the dead body of the old man who died some time ago near the main dome. Tottrr tut.. An owl made sound. Dozens of giants descended from the tree and lit bonfire. One of them went inside, brought a young naked girl and flung her on the bone fire. Then they danced around the fire with joy.

'Stop it!' He shouted with anger. The giants were stunned. No one ever objected on their cruel act before. His voice resounded in the ruins. A black shadow hovered over the giants and flew away in the sky. 'Bravo! Bravo! Young man, we salute you,' a voice came from the sky. He looked at the charred body of the girl. 'Oh no!' he shouted. A back cat passed by a dead python near the heap of the bones and skulls.

The beautiful woman escorted him to a terrace. She did not want to annoy the young man. She was surprised to see him alive. She did not know that he did not have the drink that her maid had given to him. By then she had changed her mind and had great sympathy and affection for the young man. She made him to sit at a stone bench and looked at the moon which was quite bright by then. She was looking more beautiful now then before. She was burning with some unfulfilled desire. The evil sprits withdrew into the niches of the dome. She restrained her wishes and said to her self, 'no more victims.'

The 'beauty' of the night danced in ecstasy. A band of young damsels came upstairs and joined her in dancing. They danced till the morning star Venus in the east appeared. Then they disappeared in the milky sky. Only the main beauty remained there. She sat down on the bench next to the young man and rested her head at the back of the bench. Her all vicious desires had melted down and flew away with morning breeze.

The night had gone. It was dawn. The birds had begun the morning orchestra. He got up and moved out of the ruins and came on the pedestrians track toward the village. He reached the community well. The old man was engrossed in his morning prayers. He cleaned his motor cycle and had a bath. While he was packing his luggage, the young village girl brought him some curd and said, 'Ma says that before going on a journey one must have curd. It is a good omen.' He could not say no to her and sipped the curd. He returned the empty bowl to the girl, started his motor cycle, looked at the village girl and zoomed away. The young village lass looked at him with compassion in eyes her as if saying, 'Ishtar's guest for the night please come again.'

A Date in Ruins

The biting cold and the foggy days had gone and the sun was flooding the atmosphere with welcome warmth. The plants had begun to bear new leaves and the gardens had become colourful with different kind of flowers. But Rajat's mind was filled with melancholic fog, grief and depression. He walked through India International Centre and then Lodhi Garden and came out on the road. He was wondering aimlessly just to avoid the loneliness at his two rooms flat in Rabinder Nagar. While he was passing by the India Habitat Centre, he recollected that his editor had asked him to do a feature on a young artist who was exhibiting her latest painting in Palm Court Gallery. Now he got some occupation to divert his attention from abject state of mind. He walked in India Habitat Centre and walked in the Palm Court Gallery. As soon as he entered the hall he looked around causally and his eyes rested on a tall girl with long hair worn in a plait with sharp feature and deer eyes, she was dressed up in maroon silk sari with border embroidered in pure gold thread. With her protruding tits covered tightly in frontal look gave a perfect balance to her heavy rumps at the back. Explicatively, she was looking exuberant. For a moment, she reflected the image of Bindu — a beauty Rajat lived with for some time and then he lost her in the flurry of hard time. Ever since, he lost Bindu, he was living a dejected life. The very sight of this young damsel brightened his face. She was Preetie Bhatt the Artist of the show. For a moment he forgot his agony and he ogled her for a while and wished if he could take her out in some hide out for the day to tell her his mind. He noticed that she too was responding his passionate gaze. Both were vibrating at a common wavelength, but before they could exchange words, an unwanted exigency occurred.

A coquettish and dubious woman standing next to Preetie took notice of the amorous glances between Preetie and Rajat. She pushed Preetie aside and came to Rajat.

'I am Aloka the gallery keeper. I believe you are from *The Sunday Standard.* Aren't you?'

'Yes, I am.' Rajat said and the brightness that had appeared on his face after many months was fading again.

Aloka asked him to accompany her for the coffee in the garden which had been arranged by the organizers for the visitors to the exhibition. He was reluctant to go with her. Before he could say some thing, she caught him by hand and dragged him out of the gallery. He was surprised at the guts of this woman. He was again back to his blues. In fact Aloka wanted a feature on her gallery rather than the review of the paintings by this young artist.

He uttered incoherently, 'Horrible woman.'

'Aha, did you say some thing,' the woman asked.

'No,' he said and kept on sipping coffee.

The woman tried to be friendly with him, but he was indifferent to her and after finishing his coffee he came back into the gallery.

After a long time, he resuscitated his interest in women. It was not that he was Misogynist, but he had not yet come out of the spell of Bindu. In fact he had many girlfriends and he admired, appreciated, and flirted with them, but he never had very personal interest in any of them as the memory of Bindu would come in between him and the women. Besides, no one could match Bindu. But this girl — a new discovery had really brought a change in his body soul, his mind and his imagination. Preetie was beautiful and resembled Bindu.

He talked to himself that he would not like the fish to slip out of his hand. Aloka did not want him to come back in the gallery and to develop acquaintance with Preetie. Obviously, she was a shrewd woman and had noticed what could have transpired between him and Preetie, but she could not overrule his desire and they walked together in the gallery. He saw Preetie was sitting on the counter and was busy with giving brochure of the exhibition to the visitors. He had seen the exhibition and at the moment he had no more interest in any thing except to have a word with the beauty at the counter, but he could not retrieve his courage that he had earlier to go and tell her that he wanted to speak some thing very personal. There was a conflict in his inner mind. He had come there as a journalist therefore it was expected of him to maintain all code of conduct which a dignified journalist was expected to do. But the burning flame inside for Preetie gave him a jolt and forced him to see his personal interest too. He walked up to counter and looking through and through her eyes he asked her that he would like to do a full length feature on her paintings if she could take out sometime to and see him at his flat as and when she could manage to see with the photographs or a CD of his paintings.

All through their conversation Aloka was standing and watching them with frenzy in her mind. She was jealous of Preetie. But Rajat gave dam to her and walked out with good hopes. The world has changed for him now. It was beautiful.

Rajat came back to his flat and he put his writing studio in perfect order. He picked up all papers one by one and which were of some use, he kept them in a file. He cleaned his type computer kept the pens in a tumbler, dusted the linen, his bed his furniture and after setting every thing in order, he went in the pantry, made a drink for himself and sat down in balcony and recollected his chance meeting with Preetie and tried to vie her with Bindu.

He thought of Bindu, how he met her in the dome near Kutub Minar, while he had gone to do a feature on the monuments in and around Mehrauli. Bindu was studying for Master's degree in Archaeology at Panjab University, Chandigarh and was doing a paper on the monuments of Delhi for her thesis.

'Hi! Young lady what are you doing here in these ruins — ruining your youth.'

She had a good hearty laugh and instead of replying his question, she posed a question, 'What are you doing here in these monuments? Aren't you ruining your life?'

'You hit me back with my words — very smart of you. Anyway I am Rajat – Rajat Sharma and I am doing a small feature for my paper *Sunday Standard.* But I am not in the least knowledgeable about the old monuments. These emperors — the Muslim Emperors got these buildings erected for their false ego and we have to keep them alive through our paper. May I know your name and your mission to be in the ruins young lady?'

She looked at Rajat and with a broad smile said, 'You have no chance with me. All young men try to be friendly with girls just for fun and when the girls are out of sight they forget them. Isn't so?'

'Certainly you are a difficult Beauty with capital B. For that matter all beautiful girls are difficult and vain.'

'You could have been a psychologist. Why are you hitting your head with worn structures or with fashioned stone and the crumbling walls or dome or so?'

'But gracious young lady you did not tell me your name.'

'I am Bindu — Bindu Jaipuria. Hey man! You are clever at buttering young women. Aren't you?'

'Look Young lady, what I say, I mean it and I have no intention to impress you.'

'You are an interesting character. You are not a common one.' She said with grimness on face and added further, 'I am going for a cup of tea at Tamarind. Would you like to join me?'

'Who would refuse the company of a beautiful girl? But the tea would be on me.'

'And lunch?'

Rajat took out his wallet and had a casual look what all it contained and said, 'O.K. Agreed.'

Bindu was impressed by Rajat's honesty and his frankness. She had been meeting lots of young men at the University who were boisterous and pretended to be with loaded wads while in reality they were not. But when she noticed that this young man meant honestly what he said; she developed a deep regard for him.

The two strangers walked together to a nearby restaurant –Tamarind and spent good long hours in talking to each other. Bindu was an extrovert and vocal whereas Rajat was economical in his speech. Now they were no more strangers to each other.

'Since we have come to know each other, so I shall call you by your first name,' said Bindu and asked him without waiting for his reaction, 'Rajat, would you like to have some beer?' Without waiting for his consent, she called the waiter and asked him to bring a King Fisher. 'You journalist men like drinking and eating. Isn't it?'

Rajat just smiled and said, 'No not all and not all the time. In fact people have false notions about journalists. These are not journalists only, but most of people from executive class drink a lot. Army people can not live without drink.'

While they were talking about mutual interest, the waiter brought the beer and two beer mugs. Bindu asked the waiter to bring a glass of apple juice; poured the beer in one mug and gave to Rajat.

'Won't you take beer?'

'No thank you – not today.'

'You don't drink beer or hard drink.'

'I do drink some time; but only in party or on some special occasion.'

'You seem to be from rich family. What are your parents doing?'

On this question Bindu turned her face aside and went blank. Her face became remorseful. The brightness that was dominating her personality all through the forenoon time had disappeared completely.

'I am sorry if my question has retrieved your buried unpleasant memories. What is it that has pushed you in glumness?'

She did not reply his question. She was quiet. After they finished their drink and meal, Rajat paid the bill which Bindu protested that it was she who invited him to Tamarind. All the same, they moved out of Tamarind. He left her near the Panch Sheel Club; but before they split, she asked for his address and telephone number and told him that she would be visiting in the evening. This was his first meeting with Bindu.

While he was typing the features on ruins around Mehrauli, he heard the ringing of the door bell. He left his desk and proceeded to open the door. Bindu was standing at the door with a heavy suitcase in her hand. He took the suit case from her hand and asked her to come in. He made her to sit in the living room and brought some lemonade for her to drink. He asked her if she was travelling somewhere as she was carrying a big suitcase.

'Rajat, I just met you in the morning, but my heart said to me that here is a man of my imagination who could be if not life companion but at least a friend. So I came to stay with you till my university opens after a month. I will not bother you much. I have learnt the hard way to adjust in all kind of circumstances, and if you cannot allow me to stay with you then I will have no alternative except to shift at a hotel. But one thing you promise me that you will not force me for sex.'

'Relax Bindu. How you could imagine that I will take advantage of your situation.' Rajat had a guest room which was never used except once his widow mother occupied that for a day or two last summers. He lifted her luggage and shifted it to the guest room. He opened the window for the fresh air. He kept a fresh towel, a soap cake and other necessary things like Dettol germicide tablets and walked out.

'Here is your own room. You can stay here as long as you wish. Now you go to bathroom; refresh your self and then we shall have something to eat.'

Bindu took some time to put her things in order and set the room according to her requirements. Once she had done her room, she went in the bathroom, had good shower dried her hair, dressed up and walked out and came to his writing studio, where he was busy with his article for the *Sunday Standard*. As soon as he glimpsed Bindu, he got up and asked her to tell Johan — a Goani boy what all she would like to eat. After deciding, what they would have for dinner, he asked Johan to put his drinks and some soft drink for madam in the balcony. Now they were seated and started their conversation. While Rajat was having his whisky, Bindu asked him if he could give her a strong whisky so that she may have courage to tell her sad story. Rajat smiled and gave her a Patiala peg. Now they were drinking. Bindu narrated her situation.

'I really do not know where to start from and how to start? Oh Rajat, in spite of having a father and a step mother, I am living a life of an orphan. You know, I was not even ten year old when my mother committed suicide – rather forced to commit suicide. My maternal grand father was a rich man and he left ample amount of money in my name soon after my mother's death. Though he was a noble soul, but he did a blunder by marring off my mother to a businessman. In fact, my mother was interested in another young man who was a commissioned officer in Indian Army. My father knew it, but he agreed to marriage as he was greedy and knew that mama would bring riches in her dowry; he did not love my mother. He used my mother as sex machine. I was an unwanted daughter for my father. My mother endured all kind of atrocity in bringing up me in this cruel world. I hate my mother for leaving me behind without out any consideration for my existence but I love her for her deep affection for me during her torturous time. I hate my maternal grandpa for his blunder of marrying my mother to a devil, but I love him for his wisdom to give me financial security which I needed badly.'

Bindu was terribly emotional and gulped her drink to the bottom and looked at Rajat, who reflected consonance in his eyes for Bindu. She asked him to refill her tumbler.

When he noticed that she is awfully upset, he said, 'Bindu go slow. I could imagine that you have reason to get into frenzy, but every storm is followed by rains. If you had been going through bad time, you may have good time too.'

While they were drinking, the Goan boy asked Rajat's permission if he could lay the dinner table. Rajat nodded his head and gave a small drink to Bindu and poured a small one in his tumbler.

'You know Rajat what happened this evening before I came to your place. My uncle would have raped me if I had not hit him with a paper weight that was lying on my table. While he was wiping his head, I got a chance to walk out of my room and told my aunt what her husband would have done to me. What a hell I had been through. I might have done some evil deeds in my last birth for which I am paying now.'

Rajat had a smile on his face and said, 'Bindu, there is no last birth's karma. It is all exigencies. As Jean Paul Sartre said — Life is de trop. Sufferings are fugitive so much as the pleasures are. So bear and accept the time with instinct to survive and you are doing it till now. Keep it on. Stop thinking about your bad time and let's hope you may have better things stored in life. Let's go at dinner table and have our dinner.'

At dinner table Bindu said, 'Ever since I have come here I had been talking about myself and never asked you about your family life. Who and who are in your family? What are they doing? What is your father doing?'

'My father was a senior professor of English at Calcutta University who expired a few years ago. My widow mom lives in Calcutta. She comes to see me once in a blue moon. I asked her to come and stay with me, but she does not want to leave Calcutta. I have a sister who is teaching there in a college and married to one of her colleagues. We are not rich but quite content with our life style.'

'Riches do not bring happiness. Look at me. I have big bank balance which I would not be able to consume in my life, but where is peace and happiness? You are a lucky man. How is your mother?'

'Would you like to meet my mother?'

'Yes, certainly I am keen to meet her.'

Next morning they flew to Calcutta. When he reached home his mother was surprised to see him with a beautiful girl and after they got settled she asked Rajat about the girl. He smiled and mischievously asked if she had liked her daughter-in-law. She was pretty and she liked her but he could have informed her so that she could have joined you for the auspicious occasion. Bindu felt embarrassed and told her mother that he was fooling her.

'*Maji*, we are just friend. In fact I was anxious to meet you so he brought me to see you.'

'I hope he behave decently with you.'

'More than that.'

'All right, you both relax. I shall arrange for lunch,' said the old lady and went into the kitchen. Bindu followed her and told her that it would be her pleasure to help her in the kitchen.

'Bindu, you refresh yourself. Rajat will show you the bathroom.'

Rajat was sitting quietly and was hearing the conversation between her mother and Bindu. He was anxiously waiting for an opportunity to see her mother alone so that he could tell her, that she should talk to Bindu and to find out if she could marry him. In fact ever since he had met her in the old monuments in Mehrauli, he had fallen in love with her.

He got up and asked Bindu that she must listen to mom and refresh herself. She might help her afterward.

Bindu went to bath room and Rajat got chance to see his mother in alone.

'Ma I like Bindu; please search out her mind. If she agrees, I would like her to be your daughter-in-law.'

Her mother was very happy. She had been asking him to get settled in life but he always refused to listen to her.

After lunch, she asked Bindu to join her in her bed room for afternoon siesta. So after winding up the table Bindu joined the old lady in her room. She asked her casually what she was doing and what her parents doing and what not. Bindu hesitated to tell about her parents but she did tell her about her education and her future plans. After a little informal conversation, the old lady asked her very affectionately, if she could accept the proposal to be her daughter-in-law. As soon as Bindu heard her question, posed in very affectionate manner, she put her head in her lap and began sobbing.

The old lady patted her softly at her back and said, 'My child, do not cry. If my words have hurt you I take them back. Forget about it and cheer up.'

'No *maji,* it is not that, but I am not worthy your daughter-in-law,' she said and related her family background.

'Does Rajat know all this?'

'Yes of course.'

'Then please from now onwards I am your mother as much as I am Rajat's: and now cheer up.'

In a week's time Rajat and Bindu were married off in a very modest way without any pomp and show. They flew back to Delhi as wife and husband. Bindu passed her Master's degree in good first division. But their love life did not last long. Bindu had gone to attend a seminar on wonders of the world in Canada. While she was flying back by Air India plane Kanishka, it got crashed in the air and she died with all other 360 co-passengers.

Ever since Bindu died, Rajat was living an abject life. Today after meeting Preetie, he had developed interest in life, but the memoir of Bindu obsessed him with death. He thought if Preetie also met the same fate as Bindu did, what would happen to him? He shivered and a fright sent cold wave through his spine and felt as if he was paralyzed. He poured beer in his tumbler and gulped at a stretch.

The telephone bell rang. He got up and picked up the receiver.

'Hello. Rajat on the line.'

'Mr. Rajat we found your visiting card from a young woman's purse. She met with an accident on the crossroad near India Habitat Centre. She is now in AIIMS in critical condition. Is she your relative?'

Rajat said, 'I am coming.'

He came down took a taxi and left for AIIMS. On the way, he was praying to almighty that it might be Preetie. On reaching hospital he went straight in the emergency ward. What he saw was another disaster. Preetie was dead on the table.

Mary

After getting down from local bus at Free Church bus-stop, Arisudan walked down sluggishly toward Safdar Jung Enclave. He suffered from nausea due to the acidulous, sour and stinking smell of sweating people, who were packed in the bus like sardine. Besides, he was without food since last night. He was tired and exhausted. He felt as if he would break down on the way. When he tried to restore his energy to move toward his destination, he saw a woman, who was struggling to move but could not move and sank down on the ground round the corner of the church. He forgot his own plight and rushed towards to give her a helping hand. He stood next to this woman who was suffering from acute pain. She was looking ghastly in the light of setting sun. He looked at her pathetic face. To his surprise he found it was his old time neighbour — Mary.

Bending down on her head Arisudan asked, 'Mary! What has happened to you? You are very sick.'

On hearing her name, she lifted her head and looked straight in his eyes, communicated that Peter raped her, and the acute pain swirled up like a tide in her body. Her head fell down on the ground.

Arisudan was sad to see Mary in pathetic condition. He was out to do all maximum for her in her calamity. A few years ago Mary was his neighbour in Rama Krishana Puram; and she was very helpful to him in different ways. He could not imagine that Mary would meet such a fate. He was unable to know what she was suffering from.

Arisudan got up, waved his hand to stop a three wheeler. The auto-rickshaw man zoomed and stopped his vehicle next to Arisudan. With the help of the auto driver, Arisudan lifted Mary and laid her down in the auto-rickshaw. He noticed that Mary is pregnant. He asked the auto-man to drive fast to the hospital. On the way Mary started bleeding. When the blood stains appeared on his white shirt, he could notice that she was bleeding profusely. He asked the auto driver to speed up, but the machine had its limit. Some how, they reached hospital and frantically Arisudan lifted Mary and rushed to the emergency ward. A good looking girl, perhaps she was a nurse on duty, emerged out of the side room and looked at Mary.

She said, 'Oh it is a case of maternity. She is bleeding.' She called for an attendant who placed her on a wheel-stature and moved it into the operation theatre. The nurse sat down on a chair next to the entrance door and pulled out a blank form from the table. She looked at the clock on the wall and filled in the time and date of the arrival of the patient on this form and asked Arisudan to sit down on a stool next to the table and asked him some questions.

'What is the name of the patient?'

'Mary,' said Arisudan.

The nurse asked him next question, 'Husband's name please.'

Arisudan was puzzled to hear such a question. He looked towards Mary, who was unconscious. For a while he was quiet, but when the nurse repeated the question, he said, 'I do not know.'

'Are you not her husband?' asked the nurse.

'No. I am not,' Arisudan said.

'Then who is her husband?' she asked

'It is Mary who can answer this question.'

'Is she carrying an illegitimate child in her womb?' the nurse asked.

'May be.'

'What is your relation with her?'

Arisudan said, 'Please you may enquire all these things later on. Most important thing right now is that, you please take care of the patient first. The life of the ill fated woman is more important.'

The nurse thought for a movement of some thing and asked Arisudan to sign the papers, which he did without any hesitation and without looking at, what he was signing. She got up and asked him to follow her. She moved out through a side door and walking a small distance through a corridor, she moved in to a room. A man with bald head, round face with a heavy glasses spectacle on his nose was busy with some experiment. He was the senior doctor. On hearing the squeak on the door he lifted his head and asked the nurse, 'What is the matter young girl?'

The nurse said impatiently, 'Sir this young man has brought a woman who is a case of maternity and need immediate attention.'

The old doctor said very coolly, 'Let Dr. Mohini attend it.' He plunged into his work again. The nurse wanted to tell him about the peculiarity of the case but the senior man had no time for hearing any thing further.

She asked Arisudan to go to emergency room and wait for her there. She would be back with the doctor in a short time. She hurried through corridor, reached Dr. Mohini, and told her that it was a complicated case of pregnancy and needed immediate operation.

Dr. Mohini got up immediately and moved with the nurse into emergency room. She looked at Mary and asked the nurse to make preparation for the operation.

Arisudan sat down in the visitors' room and watched them take Mary into operation theatre. He was recovering from the tension that he was suffering from, since he saw Mary on the road, but he was not out of the gravity as yet. He stretched him self with his back resting on the wall. His imaginations about Mary's pregnancy were running wild…

Marry was very a beautiful and sensitive young girl. About a year ago, when he was living in R.K Puram, Mary was very friendly with him. He was a research scholar at Jawaharlal Nehru University and Mary was a student of M.A. Social System at Kamla Nehru College. By nature, she was an introvert and could hardly mix with people. But, she was quite open with him and often spent her spare time in his small flat in studying for her master's degree or listening music or helping him in kitchen in preparing tea or coffee. At times, when the ironing man did not turn up of his own, she took his clothes for ironing. She cared a lot for him. He guided Mary in her studies and as a result of it, she topped her class in M.A. part one. Only thing that was quite upsetting to her was that her cousin Peter did not like Mary being friendly with Arisudan. Peter was a vagabond He was a dropout from school. He often gambled with street boys. But he had pleased Mary's widow mother by doing all her odd jobs, such as taking the dog to doctor when the poor creature was sick or getting the electricity bill clearance or some time getting things from market. He was jealous of Arisudan. He would create hell for Mary when she stayed for late hours at Arisudan's apartment. Arisudan would feel bad but he did not want to interfere in her family affairs. He often expressed his sympathy for Mary and wanted her to be independent after she completed her education. But it did never happen.

Arisudan completed his research work and was awarded doctorate. But with doctorate degree to his credit he was unable to get a suitable position. He was completely broken. For the last three months he could not pay his rent so the landlord threw him out of his rented flat. Mary was perturbed to see Arisudan being turned out from his flat. Mary offered him to stay in her house but Arisudan refused the kind offer. He knew that his stay with them would create problems for Mary. However he kept his luggage with Mary and walked down in the street. He was on the road without any thing to fall on at that moment. He had no idea where he was going, yet he was rambling through a bye lane and came on a road. He looked at a bus that was going to Jawaharlal Nehru University. It reminded him of a professor friend Dr. Ranganathan, who had once offered him to live in a flat at Usha Niketan in Safdar Jung Development Area. This Flat belonged to one of Dr. Ranganathan's relatives who had gone over seas for a long trip for some business; and it was lying vacant in his custody. Arisudan got into the bus when it stopped a little ahead on a bus stop.

Arisudan was suffering from a psychological inferiority complex. He had been humiliated by his landlord very badly. He was feeling as if every one in the bus was looking down on him as if he was a criminal. In reality, it was nothing as such. Who bothers for whom in this world? No one has time to think for strangers.

He got down at the university terminus and walked down towards Dr.Ranganathan's bungalow, which was not far from there. In five minutes' time he was there. He pushed the door bell. A young girl opened the door and looked at Arisudan and asked him, 'Whom do you want to see?'

'Good morning young lady, my name is Arisudan. I have come to see Dr.Ranganathan if he is at home'

'Yes he is in his library. Come in please.'

The girl was very cordial. She escorted him into the drawing room and asked him to sit there. She went away to inform her father about Arisudan's visit. She came back with a glass of water and offered him to drink. She told him that her father will join him soon.

'Thank you. I will wait for him,' Arisudan said.

'Would you like to have some tea or coffee please?' the girl asked.

He could not reply the question. In the mean while Dr. Ranganathan came in. Arisudan got up from his seat and greeted Dr. Ranganathan. Once Dr settled in a seat next to his he sat down again. Dr. Ranganathan asked his daughter to get some snacks and coffee.

The young girl brought the coffee tray and placed it next to them. During the coffee session Arisudan asked Dr. Ranganathan if the flat he was talking some months back was still vacant.

'Yes it is vacant. Do you want it? Dr Ranganathan asked.

'Yes sir I need it now,' Arisudan said.

Dr. Ranganathan got up and took out the keys from a box on mental piece. 'Here are the keys. You may shift there as and when you want to do so.'

Holding the key in his hand Arisudan said with gratitude, 'Thank you sir,' he further asked with humility, 'how much would be the rent? I cannot pay at the moment but certainly I will pay you as soon as my father sends the money.'

'You need not worry about the rent,' Dr. Ranganathan said.

'Sir, I will take leave of you,' said Arisudan and moved towards the door. When Dr Ranganathan saw him moving towards the door he called for his daughter and told her to see off Arisudan at the gate. She followed him and very courteously, saw him off at the gate. Arisudan was very intelligent fellow. He sensed that possibly Dr Ranganathan was seeing a prospective son-in-law in him. But he needed the place so he remained quiet about it. In fact he had Mary in mind.

Arisudan feelt a little better. He caught a bus for IIT gate. Then walking through Safdar Jung Development Area, he reached Usha Niketan. He had no difficulty in tracing the flat. He cleaned it thoroughly washed the floor, opened all the windows for the fresh air to gush in. After some time when the floor of the flat dried up he came down to fetch his luggage from Mary's house.

It was around three o'clock when he reached Mary's house and rang the door bell. Mary was sitting in the drawing room and was reading a novel. Her mother was resting in her bed room for siesta. Mary opened the door. She was happy to see Arisudan at the door.

'There you are. Please come in.'

Walking inside the house he said, 'Mary it is good luck. I have got a place to live in.'

'What good news! All the time, since you left I was worried about you. Have you taken any thing?' she asked and without waiting for his reply, she moved into the kitchen to make some toast for Arisudan. In a short time she brought some refreshing toasts and hot tea for him, placed on the table and in a commanding tone she said, 'Eat now. You must be starving.'

While sipping tea Arisudan looked at Mary. 'Will you come to see me at my new place?'

'Well, it will be my pleasure sir.'

In fact it turned out their last tea together. In some people's life such vicissitudes happen that their wish fulfilment never come through.

After finishing, his tea, Arisudan took his baggage down. Mary was sad to see him going. He placed his luggage in an auto-rickshaw and sat down. Before asking the driver to move, he looked at Mary, who was holding water in her eyelids and said 'Do not be sad, we shall be meeting very frequently.'

But after that Arisudan could never see her till this day when she was found lying at the road side in ghastly shape.

The clock on the wall struck. It disturbed Arisudan's retrospective mood. He was tired sitting on the bench. He shifted his posture and again got lost in his thoughts…

Once he shifted to Usha Niketan he could not find time to see Mary. He was desperately searching for some position but did not succeed. He wrote his father to send him money but to his disappointment, his father wrote back that he was sick in bed and had sold the shop to pay off the debts that he had taken to educate him. His father wrote further that he should make a visit to the village.

He wanted to go to the village with Mary as a successful man. After a few days he received a cable from his mother while he was all set to go to the office of the Union Public Service Commission, 'Your father expired. Come. Your mother Srima.'

He was taken aback to read the telegram, 'What a life! A sequence of sad affairs! Life is a perpetual struggle to get some thing, which luck turns down.' He looked at the cable again and cried, 'Oh God! Father is dead.'

Soon after appearing for his interview at the office of the Union Public Service Commission, he rushed to his village. It was late afternoon when he reached his village. People were preparing for the cremation of his father's dead body and were waiting for him.

When Arisudan reached home, the funeral procession moved to cremation ground. The corpse was placed on pyre. Arisudan was very remorseful, when he lit the pyre. People came and went away. His mother was in intensive grief. After performing all the rituals he promised his mother that he would take her to city once he gets some suitable job. He recollected her mother's image and thought of his promise to her.

Ensemble the nurse came out of the side door. A kind of glow appeared on his face to see the nurse. He thought that Mary would be fine then.

'Has Mary come to consciousness?'

'She will never come to consciousness now,' the nurse said.

Arisudan was perplexed to hear the mysterious words of the nurse.

'What do you mean by it lady? I am anxious to talk to her,' he said with an appealing look at his face. The nurse looked at his eyes which were filled with hopes and disappointment. There was a peculiar expression on his face.

‘Gentleman I am sorry to say that she died after giving birth to a boy baby,’ she said and got busy with her paperwork at the table.

He walked up to the nurse who had settled at her seat by then and asked, ‘Can I have a look at Mary?’

She escorted him to the Mary’s corpse. The attendants were preparing to send Mary’s dead body to mortuary.

He looked at Mary’s face for a moment and walked out. In the mean while there was a commotion in the emergency ward. There was a man holding a young girl on his shoulder.

‘A maternity case?’ asked Arisudan.

‘No, a rape case,’ the man replied.

‘Well Devil rules the world, not the God. God rules the heaven,’ Arisudan said and looked at the young girl on his shoulder.

‘You may be another Mary after nine months, and you will die like my Mary has died on the operation table after giving birth to a modern Jesus.’ The nurse was listening to his words. She was silent. She was also a woman and could understand the plight of a woman.

When one faces one tragedy after the other, his grief becomes meaningless. He accepted it as a fact of existence. Some live through some commit suicide. This is the way of existence.

‘What would be the fate of a commoner Jesus? Mary’s son will be son of God or son of a Devil? You can not answer my question, and who are you to answer? No one can answer. Law of existence is as such.’

Arisudan walked out of the hospital, and reached his flat. He opened the door, placed his portfolio on the table and lay down on his bed with empty stomach. He looked at the calendar to his right side on the wall with cross on the dates. One more day has passed for him. He shifted his eyesight from the calendar to the sky through an open window. Far off deep in the milky sky he saw a black spot, which was growing bigger. It changed into a woman in black dress. From other side of the window Mary's apparition appeared. The woman in black dress said, 'I am Lady Death and have come to escort Mary away from you to land of absolute freedom.'

Arisudan shook head and looked through window in the sky. A black bird was flying from a tree and disappearing in the milky sky.

'You could not protect me from Peter. But how can I blame you? You were helpless. I gave birth to a Christ — a child without father. Now I am going for never to return again. But, before going away, let me make a cup of tea for you.'

A black shadow jumped from the window and moved into the pantry. He got up and switched on the light. He saw a black cat sitting at the pantry door. He chased it away, switched off the light and lay down on the bed again.

Arisudan's imaginations were running wild. He saw a small child on foot path with an apple in his hand. A boy came on the scene and said, 'Do not eat this apple otherwise you will have a fall from the pavement into gutter.' He snatched his apple and gobbled it…

Arisudan did not know when he went to sleep. He got up when the alarm clock buzzed in the morning. He made black tea, collected newspaper from balcony and sat down on a chair. While he was sipping his tea and reading news paper, the door bell rang. He got up and opened the door. The carrier was standing with a mail in his hand.

'Here is a telegram for you sir,' he said

Arisudan opened the telegram and read. 'Mother is seriously ill — Nisha.'

He had no money to move. So he decided to sell his music system which Mary used to operate on. He took it out, went in the market sold for a throw away price and left for his village. While passing by Free Church, he looked at the spot where Mary was laying in pain yesterday evening. He thought of Mary for a while and headed for the railway station.

Regrets

Tina was planning how to bunk from the hostel, as she wanted to go for jam sessions at Hell — the most sensational discotheque of the town. Her friend Daleep was waiting for her impatiently, but she could not devise any plan. She was not an adventurous type as to tie a sari in the window and slip down in filmy style, nor was she good at cooking stories to deceive the warden. She was a very simple straightforward girl. If she had gone to warden and told her that she was going out to see her boy friend, she would have been restricted from going out for genuine outing also. So she did not know what to do with her self. While she was exasperated at her own self, her friend Dotty sauntered into her room.

'Hai Tina, what's wrong with you? You are so glum!'

Tina gave writhing smile and said, 'Dotty we are living in prison. I can't go out from this bloody hostel.'

Dotty had a grin and said 'Cool down Tina. It is very simple. You just give five rupee note to the gate keeper and you are out of the gate. Where do you want to go?'

'You know, Daleep is waiting for me in the Hell.'

'Tina, that guy is just playing with your sentiments. In fact he is not what he pretends; he is a perfidious man.'

'How dare you say such thing? I love him and he loves me.'

'If you do not listen to me then one day you will regret. I can't say more than this. As a friend and well wisher I just said the truth.'

'Dotty you are jealous of me.'

'Jealous? My foot,' said Dotty and walked out of her room in frenzy.

Tina felt bad about unnecessary exasperation for Dotty. She realized her slips of prickling babble. She got up, locked her room, came down and walked through the lobby out at the main gate. The warden was engrossed in her office work. At the gate Bahadur asked for gate pass. She was very nervous and timid but as Dotty told her she gave five rupee to the gate keeper and she was out. Bahadur was laughing at her timidity. But she did not care for it. She hired a paddle rickshaw and reached the Hell. When she entered in the dancing room, she saw Daleep clamping a girl with his arms and packing kisses on her body. Tina stood still next to him without giving an inkling of her presence to Daleep. While he was changing the position with the partner, he saw that Tina was standing behind him. He left the girl.

'Hay Tina, when did you come? I was waiting for you.'

'Waiting for me?' she asked with bitter pain at heart. She was on the verge of a break down.

'You trust me Tina. I was waiting for you anxiously.'

'Waiting for me and loving another girl?' she asked retrieving her composure.

He was a crafty man. He quickly changed the topic of conversation. Holding Tina from her arm asked her to have some coffee together. Tina could not resist his invitation. Once they settled at the table, he introduced the girl with whom he was dancing a while ago.

'Tina this is Azara. She is the daughter of an army officer and her brother is working with me in civil aviation at Safdar Jung Airport,' said Daleep. Tina had not come out of the disgust as yet, so she just nodded her head in response to Daleep's words about Azara. In fact Azara was not the daughter of an army office nor was her brother working with Daleep. She was a call girl and Daleep was her agent in getting her the customers. Daleep had told Tina that he was a pilot with an airline, but in realty he was a school drop out and had become a small timer underworld businessman. He was a drug pusher.

After the coffee, Azara had gone away and Daleep danced with Tina for half an hour. Relaxing at the Hell for some time, Daleep asked Tina to move out in an informal gathering at a friend's place. By now Tina was perfectly normal and she agreed to go with him, but asked him who this friend was.

'His name is Teddy and he works in a tea estate. He is here on holiday,' said Daleep. Tina did not ask anything further.

They came out of the Hell. Tina was feeling fresh in open air. They sauntered till a cab came and stood near by them. Daleep asked the driver if he could go to sector forty. The driver came out and opened the door to the back seat. Daleep asked Tina to get in to the cab and then he followed her. Once they were seated comfortably, the drive moved the cab. In fifteen minutes, they were at the gate of the house of Daleep's friend. Daleep paid the taxi man from the money that he had pinched from Tina's bag while she was busy romancing with him in the cab. In cab, he was embracing her with right hand and his left hand was doing the job of opening her vanity bag and taking out the cash. Then he pushed the stuff in left side pocket of his trousers. What a crafty man was he!

He escorted Tina inside the house where some freaks were tripping on hashish. The loud music was on and a few couples were swirling on the floor. He asked Tina to sit on a Davenport and walked into the pantry with Teddy.

'Who is this new chic,' Teddy asked Daleep.

'It is a big kill. But you be quiet and do not spoil my game.'

'All right yar why do you worry. Carry on with your plan,' said Teddy. Daleep took out a bottle of Cola and poured in a glass, put some white powder in it and stirred it with a spoon. He poured in another glass for himself, but it was without powder. He placed them in a small tray and came out with it. He gave one to Tina and one he picked up for himself. Tina sipped it so did Daleep. After finishing the drinks Daleep asked Tina to move in another room and got up. Tina also got up and followed Daleep. They were now in a bedroom. Tina felt a little numbness in her body and after some time she was in semi conscious state of mind and felt for sex release. Daleep made the best use of the opportunity. He had several round one after the other on her body. He was acting as an incubus, as Tina had been in swoon. When he was tired he came into the drawing room, leaving Tina alone on the bed. All the Yankees had gone and Teddy was having go-go with Azara who had come back after making business in a hotel with an Arab.

Daleep went into pantry, prepared some scrambled eggs and put into a plate with some bread slices and had hearty meal after long session of go-go with Tina. After the meal he went back to bedroom and rested for hours. It was already dawn, so he tried to wake up Tina, so that she may go to her hostel, otherwise it would be a scandal and he might be in trouble. He threw some water on her face. She opened her eyes, looked at Daleep and asked him to arrange for a cab as she must be back to hostel otherwise she would be thrown out from the College. So Daleep telephoned to taxi stand and called for a cab.

In five minutes, a cab was on the gate. Daleep pushed Tina into cab and pretentiously said, 'Good bye.' On reaching hostel, when she opened her purse to take out cash to pay to the Cab man, she found the cash was missing from the purse. She was shocked and got panicky. She asked the cab man that she would send the money through a servant; the cab man said that sahib had told me that he would pay my fare. This was a big trick of Daleep to win the trust of Tina. She walked into the hostel, and luckily the warden was in bathroom so she had no problem in getting back to her room without any problem.

But before she got ready for going to college, the warden called her and asked her, 'Where were you at the time of roll call?'

Her mind worked fast 'I had headache and had some painkillers, so went to sleep.'

Warden took her for her words and warned her, 'In future, in such situation you must send the message through the room boy, otherwise you would be fined for your absence from the roll call. Now you may go.'

Tina heaved a sigh of relief and came sheepishly out of the warden's office. She treaded for the college. She thanked to her star that no one came to know about her bunking the hostel and she is totally safe. She felt gratitude in her mind for Dotty for giving her the clue how to slip out of the hostel.

Tina's delectation did not last long. In week's time she started vomiting and felt nausea. She thought of Daleep. One day after the college was closed she went out to see him in the Hell. She knew that he was always there in the afternoon. In fact he often did his business deals in drugs at the Hell. He was talking to a hideous man, when Tina stepped in side the Hell. She went straight to Daleep.

'Oh hello, Tina, how are you?'

'Daleep I am not well ever since we met last time at your friend's place.'

'Physically I feel nausea and mentally I can not concentrate in my studies. I do not know what has gone wrong with me.'

'Relax Tina you will be alright. Let's go to Kwality for some ice-cream and we will talk over there.'

Daleep told his friend that he would see him later, and moved with Tina. In his company she retrieved her mental security, which she was missing for a few days. They had some ice cream.

After conversing on small things Tina asked him, 'Daleep why don't you talk to your father about our marriage. For how long we continue like this. If you like, I may ask my Papa to see your father and fix the time at least for our engagement.'

'Do you think your father will accept me as his would be son-in-law?'

'Why will he not accept?'

Daleep was in a fix. Though he was quite nervous, but he was a seasoned crook. He did not show it. He laughed and said, 'Tina what is the hurry? First you finish your graduation.'

'But how does the engagement disturb my education?'

'All right we will talk it over later let's go to my friend place. We will have some fun there.'

Tina was intensively in love with Daleep, so she could not say no to accompany him to Teddy's place. They came out of Kwality and hired a cab. On the way, in cab Daleep tried his craft to take out the dough from Tina's purse but ever since she lost it last time she was a little vigilant, so he could not succeed in his art, but he was a master craftsman in chicaneries.

When they reached Teddy's place and got down from the cab, he pushed his hand in his pocket pretentiously as if he was taking out some cash to pay the Tax man and uttered, 'Oh Shit! Someone had pinched my wallet in The Hell.'

'Oh my God! That place is full of pickpockets. Last time some one picked big amount of dough from my bag. But you must not worry I will pay the cab man. I have enough with me,' said Tina. She opened her purse and took out dough and paid off the cab man.

'Thank you so much Tina.'

'Don't embarrass me Daleep; it is alright.'

After relieving the taxi man, they walked towards the main gate. It was locked up and Tina noticed that unlike the previous visit it was quiet. Daleep pushed the door bell. A mundu came out and opened the gate. Daleep walked inside with Tina. He asked Tina to sit down on a settee and walked in the pantry. He was thinking to repeat the potion of some strong sedative, but after a while Tina followed him in the Pantry. He had just taken out the soft drink from the fridge and poured in the glasses, but he could not mix the white powder in Tina's glass as she had come there. Daleep thought that every thing was going wrong. He could not steal the money from Tina's bag and now he could not mix the sedative in her glass. But he kept his wits. He came out with Tina in the drawing room and had soft drinks with Tina. Soon after the drinks he asked her to move up stairs in the bedroom. Tina refused to move upstairs as she had some vague reminiscences that last time he had sex with her; though she too had felt the urge for it. But today she was in no mood of it. Daleep was a seasoned trickster and he pleaded her in such a way that after some time she could not say no. So they moved upstairs. But time was running out and Tina had to go to her hostel, so after a few round of go-go, Tina said to Daleep that she would like to go to her hostel other wise, she would be in trouble.

Daleep thought for a while and said, 'Alright you may drop me at the Hell on your way to your hostel.'

'It is fine enough. Let's go down.'

Tina combed her hair which had been in shambles during the sex-play, tide up her dress and walked down with Daleep. Daleep called for a cab and they moved into it. Tina left him at the Hell and went to her hostel. At the gate she pushed a ten rupee note in Bahadur's hand and walked in swiftly, without being noticed by the warden.

Week and a month passed and she did not have the menstruation, which created some doubt in her mind and felt as if she got some thing in her belly. She felt strongly to share her anxiety with some good friend and only good friend she had was Dotty. She often shared her secrets and personal matters with her. But she had annoyed her. She had heard from her granny that a woman starts vomiting and her menstruation stops when she gets pregnant, so she got panicky.

Putting aside her egoism, she went to Dotty's room and after apologizing for her obnoxious behaviour more than a month ago, she said, 'Dotty I may be in deep trouble.'

'What is it Tina?'

'I think I am pregnant.'

'Tina, do not have wild imagination. How can it be possible?'

'Dotty I had been having sexual relations with Daleep and my period was due a week back but it stopped.'

After a short silence, Dotty said, 'I know a doctor who is my far off relation. I can take you to him; he can do the check up and then you will come to know whether you are pregnant or not.'

'Dotty please do some thing otherwise I will commit suicide.'

'Don't be silly, you made a blunder alright, but be careful in future. And let us keep our fingers crossed, that you are not pregnant.'

'When can we go then?'

'Tomorrow, after the college, we can go to him. He has his own clinic in Sector 17.'

Next day Dotty took him to Dr. Bedi who did not take much time in checking Tina and told her that it is one month old pregnancy. After the check up they returned to hostel.

Tina was totally broken; she did not know what to do with her self. She went into her room, restored her will power and contemplated on the problem seriously. She decided to go to Daleep to apprise him of his pregnancy. But before going she wanted to see Dotty and tell her course of action. So she got up took her vanity bag, locked the room and went into Dotty's room. She was busy with her assignment; but seeing Tina she left the work and asked Tina to sit down.

Tina sat down on her bed and said, 'Dotty I want to go out to meet Daleep. I shall ask him to hurry up for the marriage.'

'Tina you will regret marrying this man. He is not a decent guy. Do not mind my straight forwardness. He has already ruined many girls before. He is a small timer underworld don.'

'How do you know all this Dotty? I know he is a very decent guy and he loves me so much that he can do any thing for me.'

'Tina, my father has a colleague — Col. Jasper, whose son was dragged in the drugs by this man Daleep. When he came to know about his son's involvement with this man he took his son to a psychiatrist who took two months to cure him. Col. Jasper informed police, but the police could not find any proof to put him behind bar. However since then he is under the surveillance of intelligence. For your knowledge his father is not an army officer. He is a petty supervisor in a construction company.'

Tina was confused; she could not believe what Dotty said to her. Though after listening to Dotty, she started looking at the other side of the situation but her sentiments for Daleep would creep in her mind. In spite of all that what dotty said, she decided to see Daleep and walked out of Dotty's room and came down.

As usual she slipped a ten rupee note in gate keeper's hand and walked out of the hostel. She had no fear of being caught by the warden. She went to the Hell. When she walked into the Hell she found Daleep whirling around with a new girl. She did not waste any time and went straight to Daleep and asked him that she wanted to talk some thing urgent.

Daleep left the girl and joined Tina. They came out of the Hell, walked in a park and sat down on a cemented bench.

'Daleep I am carrying your seed in my belly. Now you must marry me at the earliest possible time. Take me to your parents.'

'Tina, it is very simple I can take you a doctor, who will clean you in no time.'

'How can you say such thing? It is the sign of our love? No please, I will give birth to the little thing seeded in my belly. You take me to your father please.'

'My father is posted in forward areas, so it is not possible to see him at least for a year.'

'Then you take me to your mother.'

'Tina she has gone on a pilgrimage in south with my sister.'

'You are telling lies. Your father is not in army. If I am wrong then give me his address. My father will make a contact with him.'

'Tina, don't make fuss; I will take you to a doctor and get yourself clean.'

'No, you give me the address of your father.'

'If you do not agree to my advice then do what you want to do. I am a busy man. I have no time for you.'

Tina now realized that she was ruined. A man, who often said to her that he can even give his life for her delectation, was a big fraud. She could do nothing except to curse herself.

She got up from the bench and rambled out on the road. She regretted not listening to Dotty on the very first instance when she warned her of the consequences she had met. She felt like killing Daleep. After wandering around on the road for an hour she returned to the hostel and walked in her room. She was not in her normal state of mind. She did not know what to do with herself. When her thinking had come to a dead end, she went to sleep.

In the morning, Tina went to college and applied for a week's leave, came to bus stand and took a bus for Delhi. It was late evening when she reached home. Her parents were surprised to see hei coming home without any intimation to them. She told them that she was suffering from black fever so she had come to improve her health. After dinner, Tina went into her room. While leaving college, she had decided to tell the whole tragic episode to her parent, but when she reached home she changed her mind and kept the secret within herself. She was totally a changed person. Her love for Daleep had changed in to bitter hatred. She thought seriously to kill him, but she did not know how to achieve her objective. She had been thinking all wearied things. Some time she thought of committing suicide. Her weird thoughts were flowing aimlessly and she did not know when she went to sleep.

In the morning, she got up late. Her father had gone to his office. Her father Mr. Krishana Kumar was an honourable eminent industrialist of the country. She felt as if she might bring a stigma to his name. Such thoughts depressed her terribly. She had late breakfast in her room; and after the breakfast she went into her father's room. She tried to open the cupboard, but it had a special lock. She made a futile search for the key every where and while she was going out her mother came there by chance.

'Tina what are you doing here?'

'Nothing Mom, I came to see Papa, but he is not here.'

'He had gone to his office early in the morning.'

She walked out from her parent's bedroom and while she was going back to her room, her mother asked her, 'How do you feel now?'

Smilingly she said, 'I am better now.'

'Alright go and now rest. You need complete rest after the black fever.'

Though Tina said so to her mother, but inside some thing was boiling. She did not show in the least her agony and went back to her room.

Next morning, when her mother was commanding the squad of the servants for dusting and cleaning of the house and cooking, and her father was in bath room, she went in her parent's room and searched the jacket of her father. She fished out the key for the cupboard. She opened the cupboard, took out the revolver and a few rounds. She locked the cupboard as it was, kept the key back in his father's jacket and hurried back to her room. She kept the revolver and the rounds in her brief case and came down in the lobby with her small luggage.

'Mom I am feeling quite alright and want to go back to College, otherwise my work will suffer.' Tina's mother went up and told her husband, 'Krishan get ready soon and come down on breakfast table as Tinu is going back to her college.' He dressed up and came down with his wife. The breakfast table was set and all the three had breakfast together. After the breakfast He asked one of the drivers to drive Tina to Chandigarh and asked Tina, 'Do you want any money.'

'No Papa, thank you I already have enough.'

He pushed couple of thousand rupees in her bag and said, 'God bless you my darling go back and do well in studies. Bring good name to you Mama and Papa.' He came out to see her off at the gate.

In five hours time she was in her college. In the afternoon after the college when she was in her room, she took out the revolver from her briefcase and kept in her vanity bag. She had some thing drastic in her head which made her thirsty, so she took a glass of water and drank at a stretch.

Tina changed terribly. No smile no grin appeared on her face no tears in her eyes. She was no more naïve. In a few days time, she had learnt the ways of the world. She came down and as usual she walked out of the hostel without any fear of any one. She hired a three wheeler and reached the Hell. She walked very calmly inside the Hell and met Daleep with a great smile.

'You got angry for nothing my love. How are you now?'

Daleep thought that the timid dove had come to her senses and in a way she had come to her senses, but in a different way, which he could never think of. He said, 'It is O.K. Tina. Shall we move to Teddy's place?'

'We will, but what is the hurry? Let's go and have some ice cream at Milk Food. It will be from me.'

'It is fine; let's go.'

They walked out of the Hell and moved towards the Milk Food parlour which was a walking distance from The Hell.

While they were having ice cream, Tina was thinking that in a short wile Daleep will be cool for ever. They talked on light subject and once they finished the ice cream Daleep asked her to move out. She paid for the bill on the counter and came on a taxi stand. Daleep was talking to a Taxi man; Tina took out the revolver and shot at Daleep's temple from a point blank range. She kept pressing the trigger till all the rounds were empty. He was dead on the floor. She asked the taxi driver to take her to the nearest police station.

Kamayani

Kamayani was totally different from her other friends. Most of her friends were so insensitive, that they could not understand the qualities of this extra ordinary girl. They would sum up her characteristics in one way or the other and next day they would change their views about her. All had different opinions about her. When they would talk about Kamayani, I would hear their remarks on her person and would not say anything except having a good laugh – hearty laugh at their comments and then dip myself in inner self. If I uttered any word at all, it would be so abstract that they could hardly make out its hidden meanings. In fact I did not want to make any immature statement about Kamayani. For that matter I always took time in studying the mysterious characters – specially that of the girls. Personally speaking I was a women's man. So it was not the question of only Kamayani, but it was, at least for me, a matter to understand the mind of those women, who were different from those, whom I had met till then. Kamayani was very emotional, but knew how and when to control her passions. She could discriminate between good and bad characters, but her method was so different that even she would accept the vicious characters in her fold. But she was so intelligent a birdie that no one could trim her wings.

First time I met Kamayani in Chandigarh. It was Ramalania who introduced me to her as his wife. They had just come out of Shangri-La and I was passing by that place when I chanced to meet them. Kamayani had come from London and was on a brief tour of North India. Second time I met Kamayani after an interval of long five years in Delhi. She had become a mother of a child then. She was staying in a rented flat in Safdarjung Development Area. It was a chance meeting in the Wheels at Ambassador Hotel. She was dancing around with a fat young man who could not catch up the brisk movement of Kamayani. While she was swinging in her natural rhythm she spotted me abruptly. She stopped dancing and came to my table. The fat young man frenzied and did not know what to do with his own self.

'What a chance meeting after a long interval,' she said after greeting with natural warmth in her expression.

'What a contingent meeting Kamayani! I could never imagine that I will meet you. Have some drink.'

'What are you having?'

'Scotch with soda.'

'Alright I will have a small.'

I called the waiter and asked him to bring small Scotch whisky on the rocks.

While the waiter was bringing the drink for Kamayani, her dance partner came and asked her to accompany him on some other table.

In her typical style, Kamayani instead of going with him said, 'Rajan this is my new husband Mr. Parimal Minas and Parimal this is Rajan a character with a difference. Unlike you he has very strong choice of choosing girl friends. He is a mystique.'

I just said hello to this clown looking young man; then turned to Kamayani and asked, 'What happened to Ramalania.'

'Oh Rajan, he was interfering too much in my way of living so we parted.'

I did not comment on her answer and looked at her from top to bottom. She had put on a little weight. She asked me to give her pen which she noticed in my pocket. I took out the pen from my pocket and gave her. She pulled a napkin from the napkin holder on the table, jotted her new address, returned my pen with the paper and said in a commanding tone that I must see her next day at her place in Safdarjung Development Area. After she finished her drink, I asked her to have another one, but she was anxious to be back on the floor, so she pulled Parimal's hand and dragged him on the floor. They were dancing again.

I was looking forward to meet an Austrian young girl Maria, who had heard me speaking on Existentialism at the Institute of International Studies at Open University, I did not wait for her long and she clocked in at dot 9 P.M.

Maria said, 'Sir, it is too noisy here. Can we move in some secluded place?'

'Of course, we can,'

I called the waiter, paid the bill and walked out of the Wheel with Maria and moved into the lobby of the Ambassador Hotel. Once we were settled comfortably in a corner of the lobby, she asked me many questions on Jean Paul Sartre and his views that life is De trop — absurd and meaningless.

'Maria, every philosopher had grown through a particular environment which left an impact on his mental growth, and thought process. Sartre was an army officer and he saw people were killed for superfluous reasons. Hitler pushed Europe in world war. What did he get ultimately? Death. If ultimate is death of all the human beings, then all their efforts for existence are meaningless. And the alternative, what various religious communities give to mankind to make the life meaningful is to turn to God for solace. But Sartre denies the existence of all that is not factual. In fact these are not my personal views. I believe that if this life is not meaningful, then you make it meaningful. Live it beautifully till you die the natural death.'

After an hour's talk Maria went away. I also came back to my room in Panch Sheel Park. Next morning, I got up late. While I was lazing in bed, I remembered that Kamayani had invited me to her flat. I looked at the watch. It was already eleven. I knew that she was also in the habit of getting up late. So I had a leisurely bath, dressed up, made a cup of tea for myself. After the tea, I came out of the room and walked on my way to Safdarjung Development area. It was about mid day when I was at Kamayani's flat. I knocked at the door. A maid opened the door and when I entered Kamayani's bedroom I saw her giving bath to a baby. I could not imagine even in dream that Kamayani could handle a child. It was totally a different Kamayani. I greeted her in a very mild and soft voice to her and laughed to see her pouring water on the tiny body of a girl child.

'So you have adopted a child. Isn't it unlike your characteristic to handle a baby? How old is she?'

'That is true, but it has come out from my womb about four months ago in a hospital in London, so I have to bring her up.' After giving bath to a tiny little thing, she put her in a small cradle and gave her feed. After the feed the child went to sleep and Kamayani heaved the sigh of relief. She asked the maid to prepare lunch as it was nearing one o'clock. On my way to her house I had bought lots of vegetable sandwiches and patties. I passed on the packet of the eatable to her which she gave to her maid and asked her to put them in two plates and put on the dinning table. Though she had been still living a bohemian way of life, but she had added a few gazettes in her flat. She had a fridge, an air conditioner and modern furniture. Mentally she had not changed much.

Kamayani had been living in absolute freedom. As I said before she had many boy friends some she hooked for their fat purse. But certainly she was not a call girl. She had choice to make friend, if she did not like a man, she would kick him out even if he was a multimillionaire. Some were for her security reason. These ones were not hired goons. Most of them were dropouts as she herself was. So it was a relationship of coexistence. She spent on them generously, and took special care of them. She chose some of these men for her physical need. She was a nymphomaniac woman. In fact she had passion either for dancing or for rolling with men in bed. I did not come in any of the categories so I was an exception. But I really could not understand till now why she was so keen to have me at her flat. Of course to me she was a subject for my study of human psychology. So I did not mind visiting her as when she asked me to visit her.

It was unpredictable about her, when where whom and why she would pick a man for her physical need. She did not devote much time to her daughter, whom she had named Anamika. She did not have those instinctual feelings for the little soul, as a mother could have for her daughter. She was bringing her up, simply because she gave her birth. Her feelings of love had been lying deep in her unconsciousness. In spite of all such draw backs – so called draw backs, Kamayani was very helpful in practical things to those who came in her contact; she helped them with, food, shelter clothing and dough, but not with emotional fulfilment.

Once I asked her, 'Kamayani what do you think about Anamika? Do you have any ambitions for her, as to see her to become some thing great in life?'

She got lost for a few moments within her self.

'I wish I could have got Anamika aborted. So, she would not have come in this cruel world.'

Her eyes became wet. And for the first time I could see Kamayani to be so sensitive and emotional.

'Why do you think so?' I asked her

'It is true Rajan. How will she face this world? She has no father. Mother – yes she has a mother, who is a drop out from school, family and from permissive society. What will I give her tell me?'

'But you are responsible for your way of living, if you enjoy absolute freedom you have to pay heavy price for it. And for that matter who does not relish freedom in this world? Every one has to pay some thing or the other for one's existence. The only freedom is death.'

'You mean I should kill Anamika and then myself.'

'No, please do not misunderstand my words. Live the way you want to live. Relish life so far as it is there.'

'That I am doing.'

While we were involved in some serious dialogues, her boy friend Minas dropped in. She changed her facial expression thinking that he had come to take her to some restaurant or bar. She asked him to wait for some time as her maid would be coming very shortly who would look after Anamika in her absence. She had gone to market to get some milk for Anamika.

'Kamayani I have come to take you to my home. I talked to my mother about you and told her that I would like to have you in my house. And very happily she has agreed. So I have come to take you. Please pack up all what you need and come with me.'

'Minas I want to live on my own terms. Here I have my own unit and my independence. Besides after a few weeks I will be back to London.'

'We have a large house spread over one acre and you may live absolutely at your own terms in one suit with one bedroom attached bathroom a pantry and a living room. You will have a maid for your daughter and many servants at your disposal.'

After long dialogues, Kamayani agreed to go with Minas. I bade good luck to Kamayani and walked down and came to my room. I reviewed my conversation with Kamayani and found that there was a very tender person hidden in her unconsciousness. I was a mystery for Kamayani as I did not talk much and listened to her seriously. And today she was also a mystery to me. I thought that she would not go with the fat man. But when she agreed to go with him, I really revised my views on Kamayani. I was happy for one thing that at least Anamika will be looked after well. But for how long it would be was difficult to predict. But my one thesis was confirmed by the Kamayani's way of life. 'Live the life at all cost.'

Third time I met Kamayani when she was staying in a guest house in Vasant Vihar. It was again a chance meeting. It was in Modern Bazar after an interval of long six years. I had left Panch Sheel Park and was staying in Teachers' Flats near Ganga hostel of Jawaharlal Nehru University. It was a third week of December and I had come to buy some stationery in Modern Bazar. Some one shouted for me from a short distance. The voice was familiar, but I could not identify the person calling me. I turned my neck and saw Kamayani standing with a tall lean girl with sharp features at a small distance. I was surprised to see Kamayani and walked up to her. Mostly I hug my girl friends when I meet them after a long interval, but with Kamayani I did not do so. I walked up to her and stretched my hand and shook with her right hand with warmth.

'Kamayani what a chance meeting it is! Really it is so exciting to see you after long interval that I cannot put into words. When did you come and where are you staying?'

'First meet my friend Sarita Sood.' I nodded my head and said hallo to her. She addressed Sarita and said, 'Sarita this is Dr. Rajan a professor of Psychology. To me he is a mysterious person. He talks very little and listens to others with extraordinary patience.'

'I talk little as I speak so much in class that I am left with nothing to talk.' I said with a smile on my face.

'Rajan I am staying in a guest house in O-block in Street 10 House no 10. Please do come to see me as and when you are free.'

'But, most of the time you are out in Discotheque, so it will be problem to know when you are in your room and in day time I am busy at the university. If you like, we go in Sidhartha Inter-Continental for an hour or so and can exchange all we were involved in all these long years.'

Kamayani accepted my invitation and we went in into the Sidhartha Inter-Continental and leisurely walked into bar room. I asked Kamayani and Sarita if they would like to have some Indian beer and without waiting for their consent I called the waiter and asked him to get King Fisher beer for them.'

While we were sipping bear, I casually asked Kamayani, 'How is Anamika? She must have become school going by now.'

'I have put her in a boarding school, but I face problem some time, when she asks about her father. What should I tell her? She is yet small, but when she grows as an adolescent, I wonder how I would handle the situation? I changed one man after the other but no one was ready to accept the responsibility to accept her as his daughter.'

I did not comment on her expression and plunged into silence for a while. We were sipping beer in silence as if we were dumb. After a long pause, I asked Kamayani, 'Did you try to contact Ramalania.'

'Yes, I did contact, and he came a few days ago.'

'What does he say?'

'He says that biggest tragedy in his life was marrying me,' said Kamayani and had a hearty laugh. Every one in the bar looked at us.

Kamayani had the temperament to take every thing very lightly. She was aware of her problems, but she pushed them in unconsciousness. She always lived in present. She did not regret her past and did not worry much about her future. Certainly she kept herself and her accompanists in jolly mood. Besides, at times she humoured the strangers also. Every one in the bar room was grinning at Kamayani's fits of laughter. She had been very impulsive with her relationship with men folk. She was excessively extrovert and at times she would not think of the consequences of mixing around with strangers. I recollected Ramalania comments on Kamayani once when I was in Chandigarh.

'This woman mortgages her intellect for money, but as soon as she realizes her folly she pay back the money and gets her freedom back.' It took me back in past for a while and thought my last visit to her about five years ago when Minas had taken her to his house.

Once Kamayani was back to her normal self I asked her, 'Kamayani, when I met you last time, you had gone to live with your friend Minas. What happened to him? You are not staying with him this time. Is it because Sarita is with you?'

'No Rajan. He is bloody bastard — a motherfucker. You know he wanted to share me with his friends, so I gave him a good kick on his pan, packed my luggage took Tanya and went away to London.'

I grinned at her abusive language and her treatment to Minas, but soon after I got in my serious mood; and contemplated at the ambivalent characteristic of Kamayani. It reaffirmed my views about her that she was not a whore and a weak woman. She knew herself well and was capable to protect her self in all kind of situations. I had developed admirable feelings for her.

We both had been talking for long and Sarita was a silent listener to our conversation. Quite tall in height lean in body, with her tits projected excessive and her thin waist — all together made her very impressive young girl. Indeed she was nifty. I asked Kamayani, 'Is Sarita like you as a freedom loving girl? Is she also drop-out from school?'

'No Rajan, she is very different kind of a person. She is doing her masters degree in Psychology from London University and she is on vacation. In London she is my neighbour and I often talk to her about you. A week ago we went to your flat in Panch Sheel Park. It was locked up. So we returned disappointedly. But what a luck! I could never imagine that we would meet like this.'

I asked Sarita, 'What are you specializing in psychology?'

'I'm specializing in Existential Psychology.'

'It is very interesting subject. Will you go for doctorate after your master's degree?'

'If I do well in my master's degree, I may possibly go for doctorate.'

'Are you not sure about your doing well?'

'We cannot be sure of any thing in life.'

I changed the subject and asked her, 'Are you interested in visiting historical places like Agra's Taj Mahal.'

'It all depends on Kamayani, if she comes with me I will certainly go.'

'Sarita take your independent decision. I'm more interested in meeting my old pals in discotheques.'

He said casually 'Sarita, I just asked you as some of my students at the Jawaharlal Nehru University were planning a trip to Agra and Khajuraho, so I thought that if you wanted to visit these places you will have the company of likeminded people.'

'When are they going?'

'They will be leaving on December 24 and would return on January 2.

'How can I join them?'

'You come tomorrow to School of Social Sciences and I will introduce you to them.'

After an hour, we dispersed. Next day Sarita went to Jawaharlal Nehru University. She did not find any difficulty in reaching me. I took her to the common room and introduced her to one George the in-charge of extracurricular activities, and told him that Sarita would like to join them in their forth coming tour to Agra and Khajuraho. I left her with George and came to my room.

Sartia had a superbly good time during the tour of Agra and Khajuraho. She visited me on January 3, 1980. She commented on the nudity in the prolific embellishment of Khajuraho temple.

I asked her, 'Which of the two types of buildings — Taj Mahal or Khajuraho Temples you liked the most?'

'Both are beautiful in their own ways. Taj is the expression of grandeur and romanticism, where as Khajuraho expresses the love of body soul and the rhythm of life.'

I did not comment on her remarks, but certainly I admired her intelligent comments. Sarita was the student of Psychology so I did not want to give any chance to her to know about my mind. I liked her and wished to get settled with her in life, but I did not want to be fast. I really did not want to lose her, but now it was a big riddle for me to tell her my mind.

After a few days, Kamayani came to see me in my study room and said, 'Sarita loves you, but she fears to confess it in front of you. She thinks that you might reject her. Though she was born and brought up in London, but she is very shy type of a person. She heard a lot about your qualities from your students and ever since she has returned from the tour, she has become very reserved. She has become a dreamer.

'Please tell her to see me before she leaves for London. When is she going back to London?'

'She had come for two months but now she wants to go back as soon as she gets a seat in the plane.'

'Tell her to see me tomorrow.'

Day time passed in the books and papers, but the night was terrible. I could not have a comfortable sleep. I really liked Sarita, rather I had amorous feeling for her and I wanted to have her as my life partner, but when it was maturing in reality I doubted my own self. At least she has Kamayani to talk out her heart; I have no one to speak out my feelings. That night I might have slept not more than an hour. In the morning when I reached office I had a terrible headache. I had some aspirin and after taking my class I retired in my room. At about 10 o'clock Sarita came. We greeted each other and I asked her to follow me as I came out at the parking lot, opened the door of my fiat and asked her to get into and steered it to Essex bar. We both were silent in the car except exchange of few words on weather and driving conditions in India.

In Essex we got settled at a table in a dark corner. I asked her, 'Sarita what would you like to have?'

‘Nothing please. I had the breakfast just before coming to you.’

I asked the boy, ‘Bring something for the Madam and then I will tell you about myself.’

Smile appeared on Sarita's face and for a while here sobriety disappeared.

He asked the boy, ‘Get two whiskies — one large and one small and a plate of French slices.’

After a short pause, I asked Sarita, ‘Who all are in your family and what do they do?’

‘I live with my parents. My father is a Professor of History at London University and my mother is a housewife. I'm the only child of my parents.’

While we were talking to each other, the waiter placed drinks and the French slices at the table. I gave the small glass to Sarita and took the large for myself and after saying cheers, I took a long sip. Sarita took it reluctantly. I gave her moral support and said to her that she was on a holiday so she must break the minor rules. I knew that a person speaks the truth once he or she is drunk: so I wanted to know her true feelings for me. We had another round of whisky. It did well to me and the feelings which were hidden under some unknown fear rose up in mind. I said to her, ‘Sarita, the way you think about me I also think the same way for you. In my twenty two years of matured life I never met a girl of my choice. Not only I like you but I love you and I love you immensely. Tell me honestly, do you love me?’

‘Sir, I too love you, and I would not have confessed it if I would not be sure of your feelings.’

‘Sarita, we will wait for each other till you do your post graduation. If you still have the same feelings for me as you have at this moment, then we will get married. In the evening at about 8 o'clock, you come with Kamayani to my flat near Ganga Hostel. We will have a small ceremony.’ After the drinks and lunch I took her to Tanishk Jewellers. I bought two rings and drove back to her to the guest house. I kissed her on her neck and wished her good luck.

In the evening, I invited my friends and a few colleagues for a small party. The entire catering was done by the Essex. Sarita came with Kamayani. Luckily my mother was staying with me. She received her with all religious ceremony. At about 9 o'clock, the ring ceremony was performed. Next day she went away to London.

Last time I met Kamayani, at the guest house of Dhirendra Brahmchari. She had a great transformation in her life. I visited her with Sarita. According to Sarita's wishes we had adopted Anamika as our daughter at the time of our marriage a few years ago. That was the last seeing of Kamayani. No one knew where she had gone after she left Brahmchari's Ashram.

Last Days of a Dancer

'Trin-trin trin-trin trin-trin trin-trin!' The telephone was ringing for some time when Karan was disturbed in his sweet slumber by the sharp and loud and loud pitch of the beetel in one corner near the bar room in his house in sector 4 at Chandipore. He got up from the rocking chair where drinking Grant he did not know when he fell asleep. He fumbled incoherently, 'Who the hell was ringing so early in the morning?' He staggered to the phone and said in slurred voice, 'Hello.'

'Hi! I'm waiting on the station for you to escort me to town,' a female voice came from the other end of the line.

'Ouch! I am sorry, I could not reach the station to receive you in time however I shall be there very shortly.' He placed the instrument on the cradle and walked out in the garden.

Lacchu — the house keeper and his wife were in the kitchen and were waiting for him to get up so that he might be served the morning tea. Mela Ram — the driver was sitting on the garden bench near the mango grooves and was sipping Darjeeling tea, Kanta Prasad, the gardener was milking the cow near his cottage in the corner of the estate and his wife Gauri was brushing off the flies from the cow so that it may feel comfortable.

Karan yelled for Mela Ram, asked for the Key of the Honda car keys and told him to set the guest rooms in perfect order as some guests are coming from Bombay.

He went in the garage, took out the car and zoomed off for the station. While driving, he pondered on the strange situation that caused him to forget going over to the station in time. In his deep sleep he was dreaming as if he was driving Manjusha in the hills. A donkey was standing still in the middle of road. He had nearly bumped into the creature. He wavered safely. He muttered, 'Idiot! What is it doing standing quietly on the road?' He got lost again in the pleasant thoughts. He was playing hide and seek with Manjusha in the thick forest in Nagar. He was fleeting after her in the air like a Cupid.

Any way he will be meeting her in real life after a while. He reached the railway station, parked the car near the retiring room and walked into the waiting room and looked at Manjusha excitedly.

'I am sorry I kept you waiting due to some peculiar reasons I could not reach you in time,' said Karan.

Manjusha was upset. 'It is alright,' she said in low tone.

Manjusha had come with her mother Shobhita and two accompanists. He walked out of the room and called for the coolies and asked them to carry the luggage out.

They were travelling with heavy luggage and musical instruments that would not fit in his car, so realizing the gravity of the situation Karan called for a station wagon. The coolies stuffed the luggage in the wagon. The accompanying musicians and Shobhita got in the wagon. There was no space left for Manjusha in the wagon so Karan asked her to come and sit next to him in his car.

Seeing Manjusha sitting with Karan in his car, Shobhita descended out from the wagon and hurried to Karan's car. Karan did not like, but he did not express any thing and opened the back seat door for her to get into the car. He instructed the driver of the wagon to follow him and drove back home. There was silence between them till Karan said, 'I have some proposal for you Manjusha.'

Manjusha looked inquisitively at his face. 'What is it?' she asked.

'I may arrange for your performance in other cities like Jallandhar and Jammu, if you are interested in it.'

'Well, I'm not in the proper frame of mind; let me have some time to think of it,' she said.

'I can understand. Long journey and then tomorrow's function may be taking toll on your mind.'

'Nothing as such please.'

Again silence prevailed till they reached Karan's house. He had a palatial house with four large well equipped spacious bedrooms with attached bathrooms. A large drawing room furnished with imported furniture. It had a huge kitchen. On the first floor there were two large guest rooms each attached with aristocratic bathroom. The rooms opened towards the Shiwalik hills in a verandah. On the three sides of the main building, there was a sprawling lawn with well trimmed lush green grass. Along the boundary at the back, there was a large mango grooves. In the southern part of the plot there were workers quarters. He had a large squad of workers to look after his establishment.

As soon as the gatekeeper opened the gate, Lacchu, Mela Ram and Kanta Prasad rushed to unload the luggage. He instructed Kanta to lodge the musicians in the annexe; and asked Lacchu to take Manjusha's and her mother's luggage to the guest rooms.

After giving his servants all detailed instructions, he accompanied Manjusha and her mother inside the main building. He made them relax in the drawing room. In the meanwhile Paro — Lacchu's wife served them cold drinks in style.

Karan went upstairs and inspected the guest room and found them perfect to his satisfaction. When he came down in the drawing room, Manjusha was conversing with her mother on some incident that had occurred in the train, but seeing Karan's obstruction became abruptly quiet. Thinking that they need privacy, he escorted them in their rooms and came down.

Both Manjusha and Shobhita had room of their own. This was Manjusha's first visit to Chandipore. She was surprised to notice the life style of Karan; though she had been meeting him in Taj as and when he was in Bombay. But he never showed off his riches as such.

She went into the bathroom, stripped off, looked at her well maintained body and thought of Karan. I am a dancer and Karan admires my performances. But he never showed interest in my body. He never said I'm beautiful. He is an idiot.

Thak Thak! There was knocking at the door.

'I am in bathroom,' she shouted.

'M'm please come down for the breakfast after the bath. Sahib is waiting for you.' Paro was at the door.

'Alright! It is alright!' Said Manjusha and lifted her body in water tub. There was foam all over her body. She took some time to come out of the tub. She wiped her body and watched her nakedness. 'I'm sexy! Mohit is good but Mama does not like him, simply, because he is a failure in celluloid world? But sex release is also the part of life. Well Karan…'

There was again knocking at the door this time it was her mother. She said loudly, 'Manjusha why are you taking so long? Come down Karan is waiting.'

'Please you go I will come after some time.'

She dressed up in pink top and purple skirt. After doing her locks, she looked in the mirror at the dressing table. She sprinkled Lady's Pride at her body, put on the Woodland high heals and walked out. She descended into the drawing room and looked at Karan and gave him a mysterious smile. Though Karan responded but was not vocal. She walked towards the dinning table where her mother was waiting for her. Karan also got up and joined them at the table. He was reading *The Times.* It had carried a feature on Manjusha. He handed over the page to her. She glanced at it but did not show any excitement.

Except the weather and the comfort of rail journey, nothing much transpired between them at breakfast table. Manjusha and Shobhita relaxed in their room. Karan's secretary Silvia had come. They went into his office behind the main building. He dictated her a few letters and then asked her to go to the office of the Indian National Theatre after typing the letters on the computer and find out how many tickets for next day's function had been sold. He wanted that the hall must be full so that the performer got morally boosted up. He opened his laptop and read the e-mails. Most of those were crap. He deleted them and then answered the very personal one.

He had invited the important people of the town for the dinner given in honour of Manjusha's visit to Chandipore. Apart from the Governor Mr. B.S. Adhikari and a few ministers, most of the invitees' were university professors and the senior bureaucrats. Manjusha had never attended such a grand banquet before in her life. She dressed herself in the best of her attires. She wore green silk sari with golden border. She carried herself beautifully. She met many young men who tried to glue to her like honey bee. Journalists were running around her and shot the volleys of questions. Camera men were hounding her with frequent glares of light. People relished the best of wine and food. At about eleven o'clock the guests receded away and she retired to her room. Her mother felt tired and slept soon after she crashed on the soft bed. Manjusha slipped down and came to Karan's bedroom. She gave him a bear hug. Karan asked her to hold herself back for some time.

'Is there some thing physically wrong with you?'

'Nothing is as such. We will talk about it later. You go and sleep. Tomorrow is very important day,' he said.

She went away in her room.

Karan restrained himself with much difficulty. He was on the verge to... He had kept a secret away from most of the people that he had a woman in London who had swindled him and blackmailed for some time. After a few months he would be a free man.

Next day Manjusha got up very late. And after the breakfast she walked over to the musicians for a brief rehearsal. Her mother never left her alone, which she did not like. She followed her in the annexe.

In the evening, Manjusha gave a heart throbbing performance at Rabindra Rangshala. She captivated the audience. After the performance Karan pecked kisses on her cheeks.

In the morning he went personally to leave Manjusha and Shobhita at the airport.

He said to Manjusha, 'We will be soon together. Take care of yourself. Love.'

He packed the musicians by train.

Karan went to London and finalized the matter legally after paying the devil's share once for all to the woman who had been sucking his blood.

Soon after returning from London to Chandipore, Karan telephoned Manjusha. Her mother picked the telephone. She asked him to come over to Bombay. So he took the earliest possible flight for Bombay. He booked himself at Taj. Once he was settled in his suite, he telephoned Manjusha. Her maid picked up the telephone, who told him that the young madam had gone to Goa with her boy friend Mohit. Karan put the receiver on the cradle.

He got a big shock. But he was a seasoned man and kept himself integrated. In fact he had developed a great fascination for Manjusha. Next day he telephoned her again. This time Shobhita picked up the telephone. 'When is Manjusha returning from Goa?' he asked.

'Who told you that Manjusha had gone to Goa?'

'Your maid.'

'Oh! The silly girl does not know the reality. She has gone to Pune to see an ailing aunt. As soon as she comes, I will ask her to contact you. I believe you are at Taj.'

'Yes, I am located at Taj.'

Shobhita told him a white lie, and scolded her maid for the information about her daughter that she had given to Karan. Karan stayed in Bombay for some time. One day an acquaintance Maya Abrol bumped into him while he was drinking Johnny Walker in a Bar Room. She knew that he had intensive liking for Manjusha.

'Hello Prince! I met your dancer girl at a beach in Goa while she was fooling around with one yesteryear's low grade actor.'

Karan did not comment at her statement and kept quiet.

'Would you care to join me for a drink,' he asked Maya.

'Thank you. I will relish Jin with Cordial lemonade.

'Bring one large Jin with Cordial lemonade for my friend,' Karan said to the bar boy.

They talked about light affairs in life. In the meanwhile Karan asked her, 'Have you any idea when Manjusha is returning to Bombay.

'Maybe tomorrow.'

After a few days when Karan was checking out to catch an Indian Airlines plane for Chandipore, he received a call from Manjusha. 'Oh Karan, I have just returned from Pune. Mama told me that you have come to see me. Please I will be coming to see you.'

Karan did not like her telling lies. However he said, 'In half an hour I will be going to Airport to catch a plane for Chandipore.'

Frantically she walked out from her house and took a cab for Taj. She caught him while he was getting into a cab. After releasing her cab she dashed into him. She gave a broad smile,

'You may come with me to airport. We may have time to exchange a few words.'

Karan did not tell her that he knew that she was lying about her visit to Pune. He had lost his enthusiasm about her, though deep into his heart he had loving feelings for this young dancer.

'Can't you postpone your journey. Let's have some time together.'

'I can't, as I have some urgent business in Delhi. However I will telephone you from Chandipore.'

They reached the airport. He gave sufficient money to the cab man and told him to take madam where ever she wanted to go. She came out to see Karan off, who quickly checked in for his flight.

Karan did not telephone Manjusha. In fact he avoided purposely but this did not mean that she was off from his mental screen. For some time he went on receiving the call and mail by post from her, but then the communication stopped.

Manjusha had completely changed. She despised Mohit. She felt guilty of deceiving Karan. Earlier she was keen to have sexual relation with Karan, but now she adored him. But Karan did not know the change that had taken place in Manjusha.

After fifteen years.

Karan had come to Bombay to see an ailing friend who was his house mate in London. Karan had checked into Taj. One day when he was in the Bar Room, he confronted Maya Abrol. She had grown wrinkles on her face, but she had put heavy make up to hide them. She looked hideous.

'Oh! How are you young lady?' She was drinking whisky.

'Well life goes on.'

He sat down next to her and ordered a long Johnny Walker.

'How are you prince? Have you heard that you dancer friend was in coma.'

'What happened to her?'

'No one knows what has happened to her. First she lost her mother then she fell sick. Over a few months she is speechless and is kept on liquid food through pipes.'

Karan finished his whisky and went up in to his room. He picked up the telephone and dialled her number.

The operator in the exchange explained him, 'The number is changed he should put 2 before the old number,' Karan followed the instruction and dialled again. This time it started ringing.

'Hello! Is it the number of Manjusha?'

'Yes, but she cannot speak.'

Karan asked for a cab and went over to see Manjusha. He was cursing himself for his hard and pretentious attitude towards her. In fact at no stage he had stopped thinking of her. He was in love with this woman. Every time his well wisher asked him to get settled he turned down the offers as he loved Manjusha.

He reached her house in fifteen minutes' time. He did not face any problem in locating her place. When he entered her house the old maid told him that she can recognize his acquaintances but she cannot speak. After briefing him for a while, she escorted him to Manjusha's bed where she had been fed through a pipe in nose.

When Karan looked at her face she recognized him and surprisingly the tears flooded from her eyes and trickled down her face. She still had the same old glow on her face. Karan kissed her cheeks and sat next to her still body. He spent a couple of hours with her. In the evening before leaving her house he asked the old maid if she slept like normal people.

'No, she is always awake.'

Karan visited her every day and spent his day time at her bed side for a week. But he had to come to Chandipore as he was involved in many charitable projects.

Before leaving Bombay, he asked her doctor, 'Do any of her relatives visit her.'

Unfortunately after her mother's death I have not seen any of her kin's. Since she was the dance teacher of my daughter whom she loved immensely, so I take care of her. In fact before she fell sick she had transferred her bank account in my daughter's name, which we will use for charitable purposes.

'For how long she is in such state of health?'

'For the last four months I am seeing her in such condition.'

'Is there any cure for it?'

'That will be a miracle.'

'Dr.Vasudeva I have to go back to Chandipore for some charitable urgent work. Please, if any thing happens adversely, give me a call on my mobile.'

After fifteen day, Karan received a call in the morning, 'Hello sir Manjusha has got mukti.' She had breathed her last a while ago.

'Dr. Vasudeva I am coming from first available flight. Do not cremate her.'

Karan reached Bombay by 2 P.M. and did the last rites for Manjusha. He stayed there for all the formalities that were required according to Vedic religion. All these days he contemplated on the last few days that he spent with Manjusha.

Sharabni

Bhupen Roy was engrossed in scripting the foreword for the exhibition of his new paintings at Ark Art gallery. Suddenly a woman in her thirties popped in his studio and asked him if he could spare some moments for her. He glanced at her curiously. She was dressed up not very gorgeously in nylon sari with bold and large floral print on sky blue background. She was not short; with single structure, she looked fragile. With thin midriff, she was looking figure conscious. There was some pathetic look in her eyes. He asked her to come and sit on the chair across the table. She wobbled around and settled on the chair.

'Who are you and what has brought you here young lady?'

For a moment she looked down at her vanity bag desolately and fumbled, 'I am Sharabni Mondol and I need a remunerative position desperately.'

'What contingency makes you so desperate for a placement?'

'Well it is a long story.'

She looked for time at the watch at the wrist and babbled abjectly again.

'Please do something for me.'

'Be at ease. Would you like to have something — tea or coffee?'

'Thank you so much, plain water will do.'

He pressed a button on beetel and asked the care taker for water and two coffee.

'Please give me your resume,' Bhupen asked her.

'I do not have any such experience but here is my bio data which contains my qualifications etc.' She handed over a typed page to Bhupen.

'So you are from Calcutta,' looking at the paper Bhupen said.

'Yes, I am originally from Calcutta.'

Toto came with a tray of water and coffee. He moved the key board aside to make the space for the coffee tray. She placed the tray on the table and asked if anything else was to be presented.

'No thanks, you may go now.'

Looking benignly at Sharabni, he asked her to pick up the tumbler of water. By then her anxiety had lessened and had recouped equanimity. She picked up the tumbler and sipped it at ease and after drinking the water; she placed the glass back on the tray and picked up the coffee mug. Bhupen was already sipping his coffee. After coffee, Sharabni was off. Of course before she left his office, he assured her that some thing would be done for her. He evaluated the whole preposition and put her resume in his diary.

At about one o'clock, Bhupen wound up his papers and got up for the lunch break. He came out of his Studio and came on the road to his Maruti 800. He opened the door, got onto the driver's seat, and zoomed away for home. While he was passing by a bus stand near the IFFCO square he spotted Sharabni at the bus stop. Possibly she was waiting for a bus to go to her place. He stopped the car and shouted for her. She then saw him and rushed to him.

'Where are you going?' asked Bhupen

'My house.'

'Where is your house?'

'In Maruti Vihar.'

He opened the front door and asked her to jump in. Once she was seated properly, he asked her to guide him the way to her house. After dropping her at her house, he came home and after lunch went for a siesta. While he was relaxing in his bed, he thought of his girl friend Deepti whom he had lost to an accountant — a dry man. He had practically forgotten her, but the pathetic look of Sharabni made him to contemplate consonantly on Deepti.

Next day on reaching office, Bhupen telephoned one of his friends about Sharabni for a placement; who immediately conveyed him to send her to his creche where a maid is required on regular basis. He took out Sharabni's number and dialled her, 'Hello Sharabni you are lucky. You may join the Geetanjli Creche with immediate effect. You will be paid more than your expectation.'

Bhupen was a seasoned man and his crave for women had subdued. Of course he was always ready to stand by the delirious ones. Now Sharabni got a placement so he forgot about her. But after a week ever since he met Sharabni, when it was Bhupen's aperitif time in the evening and was taking his favourite Red Label with honey and lemon, some one pressed the call bell.

'The door is open, please walk in,' he intoned

Bhupen never liked any intrusion in the evening during his drinking session. No one at home disturbed him in his solitariness in the evening. For many years virtually he had been sitting in his bar room and drinking for hours together and contemplated on his yesteryears. Some people thought that he was eccentric. If any one would have come at that juncture he would feel very uncomfortable. But he would not show his indignation. Today after a long time, he did not detest the visitor. Of course he was not very elated to see the newcomer.

'Good evening Mr. Roy.'

'Oh! Sharabni! Good evening. What a surprise! Come on. Sit down.'

'I have come to express my gratitude for your timely help,' sitting on a cane chair Sharabni said.

'This is alright. What would you like to have? Do you take strong drink?'

'I do drink liquor, some time.'

'I have whisky, gin, beer, French wine, choose any thing.'

'Gin with lemonade will do.'

Bhupen was surprised to see this courageous dame who walked in his house without prior appointment and when he asked her for her choice of drink she asked without hesitation for gin. Of course it had become fashion with Indian women to have hard drinks. Ensemble he turned his hand to a bottle of gin, then lemonade and tumbler lying in his bar and made a large drink for Sharabni.

Stretching his hand with gin in tumbler towards Sharabni, he said, 'Here is your drink. Enjoy it.'

'Thank you sir, you are very generous.' Bhupen evaded her remarks and lipped his whisky. For some time they were silent. For Bhupen this is the time when normally he enjoyed drinking in silence. But it was exigency of the moments to be a good host to the visitor. Besides, it was embarrassing to be dumb in front of a nifty woman, so he burbled.

'How did you trace out my residence?'

'I telephone your office. And found out the address.'

'Ah! You are clever. Women from Calcutta are resourceful.'

'Do you think so?'

'Well I am talking about the well educated women.'

'In man dominating social system, women are treated as sex machine; they are not beyond the factory to produce children. It is universal fact.'

Sharabni said exasperatedly and gulped her drink at a stretch and kept the glass at the table.

'Please may I fix another drink for myself?'

'Sure.'

Bhupen was stunned to hear the unexpected and undeterred utterance by Sharabni. He sensed some truth in her utterance. He guessed that she might have been assaulted terribly by some misogynist or was jilted in love affairs. He looked at Sharabni, who had by then made a drink for herself and was gulping it.

'Hold yourself; please go slow. I think someone has injured you mentally.' She felt consonance in his words and started sobbing. Bhupen could assess the flurry she was going through, but he did not know the exact mishap she might have gone through.

'I think you have gone through some tragic mishap. I may possibly be helpful to you in your torment; if you speak it out. And even if I am unable to help you, at least it will release your pant up aggrieving emotions,' he consoled her.

'Life is de trop.'

'You have read Sartre?'

'Not very much?'

'You have used his phrase.'

'I volunteered to get trapped in false allusions. Now I regret.'

'You are very quizzical. Tell me in straight forward manner. What all and how all had happened to you?'

'I loved a man Mr. Ajit Mondol (rather he loved me) and married him against the disapproval of my parents. Before marriage he bragged to stand by me through thick and thin, and I believed him. Not because I was ignoramus, but I was deep in love with him. After a few years of marriage, her mother taunted me that I had trapped her son and deprived him of decent bride with immense riches in dowry. She always tried to cook some excuse or the other to humiliate me. Since Ajit was under the strong influence of his mother so he never rescued me against his mother's atrocity. He turned out to be an utterly sheepish man — a spineless creature. She was a bloody bitch. One day when I was feeding Kunal (my son), she tried to slap me for no rhyme and reason. I caught her hand and twisted it. Ajit, who was standing and watching, slapped me. I slapped him in return. He had a shock of his life. I had no one to stand by me except my little child Kunal. After a few days of this incident, I received a notice of the divorce case that Ajit had filed in the court of law.'

'It implies that women are enemy of women. Don't you think Sharabni?'

'To some extent it is true, but then, these are men who create such situation. Why did Ajit support his mother against me? Isn't it injustice?'

'Had you introspected yourself and found that you still love Ajit?'

'I hate Ajit. What didn't I do for that man? I defied my parents; I discarded my family — my community and walked out of my home with him. And what did he do? Ah! I hate him, I hate him, I hate him...'

'I can understand your indignation. How is your father's reaction to your situation?'

'My father though supports me. But time and again he says that my marrying a low cast man has left indelible blot on the Mukharjis' family. He has no consonance for me. He stands by me simply his prestige is at stake. For him I am an object not a subject. He is a typical austere Brahmin for whom women are appendages to men. Of course he supports me in my stand against the Mondals, but certainly he would have withdrawn his support had I married to a Brahman boy. Mondols are low caste people. Father hates Mondols. That is another evil in the Brahmnical system.'

'What's about your mother?'

'My mother? Oh God! She has no say in the social affairs of the family. But in heart of heart she loves me.'

'Is your father a businessman?'

'No, He is a chemist.'

'Well off?'

'Very well off. But I never asked for any financial help. Till late I have been selling off my jewellery to support myself and now with your timely help I got a job.'

Sharabni emptied her glass and fixed another drink for herself. She was getting binge. Bhupen sluggishly looked at Sharabni with a little apprehension that she might not feel sick or might behave fatuously as she was at spree with her drink. But he did not stop her. He was confident of himself to abate nuisance if she indulged in after being deadly drunk.

'Since when you have become alcoholic?' whimpered Bhupen.

'What an absurd question you posed Mr. Roy.' She gurgled truculently and drained the gin in her mouth. Bhupen grinned and asserted, 'You couldn't grasp what I intended to incite. People drink some time to drain out their grief and miseries. Is it so with you?' Bhupen asserted with a mysterious smile on his face.

'I don't know. Ump, may be... Mr. Roy, can I spend the night at your place?'

'Relax young lady. Relish your drink.' He picked up the tray of dry fruit and offered her. She picked up an almond and when tried to drop in her mouth, it fell down on the floor.

'Oh shit how clumsy I am?'

'Do not contrite Sharabni. Tell me, what would you like to have for dinner? Your choice is limited to vegetarian preparation.'

'Any thing will do, except human meat.'

Bhupen had a good laugh at her answer. But later on, he realized that there is deep meaning in her words.

'You have very sensible wits.'

'Thank you. You are really a love.'

Bhupen yelled for his house keeper, who was crinkling the pans and plates. He left the kitchen chores and walked out in the bar corner of the living room. Looking at him Bhupen said, 'Joe, please set the table for the two people. Madam will join me for dinner.'

'Yes Sir.' Joe said and receded back to the kitchen.

Sharabni was so pinged that she could not speak coherently. She blurred, 'Cn I oz ur telet?'

'You mean toilet?' Bhupen confirmed.

'Yah.'

'Please do go. I will escort you?'

Sharabni got up and staggered, but she was not in a position to balance her steps. Bhupen held her arm and took her to bathroom. Once she was inside, she fiddled with her zip to untie her panty. She could not do it. Thinking that she had done, she pissed in her panty and yelled for Bhupen to give her hand to walk out of the bath room. Odd situation. It was embarrassing for him as she wetted her pants. He yelled for Joe and asked him to call his wife to handle the binged woman.

Rebecca (Joe's wife) escorted Sharabni to bed. She laid her at the bed in guest room, removed her wet clothes and dressed her in Bhupen's night suit. Soon after she was off to sleep.

After dinner Bhupen walked into her bedroom and had a close look at the young woman who was muttering in deep sleep. Bhupen tried to make out what she was muttering but it was too incoherent to understand any thing. She was looking beauteous in the defused light of bed side lamp. In spite of her fatuousness, he had developed liking for her — rather he grew loving feeling for her. Bhupen was a very sensitive and debonair man; he never showed his feelings for women. She was sleeping well and once he reassured himself that she would be alright in the morning he came out in the living room, fixed the davenport and laid down on it.

Sharabni was heavy on his mind. He was reviewing her plight objectively. She had valid points to be bitter about the ways of the world, but still she had some spark in her darkened mind that made her to fight out the odd she was facing. He admired her mental strength. She was justified for her stand in life. She trusted Ajit and discarded everything for him. She was a great lover. I could understand why she was drinking recklessly. He got up from the bed and walked in the bedroom again. He ogled her. An erotic tide in mind created a conflict — restraint or no restraint. 'No! No, I do not want to become an incubus.' He felt contrite and walked away.

He did not have sound sleep. Many complex thoughts had slipped through a small slit in his mind and kept him busy in analysing his own inner self. He got up early in the morning and after alighting in toilet, he popped into the bedroom to glance at Sharabni. She was still in deep sleep. Then he went into the kitchen and fixed a lemon tea for himself. He walked out in the back yard lawn with the cup and sat down on a garden chair. While he was sipping tea, he thought of the evening scene. He often went for a walk in the morning but today he cancelled it as he had a peculiar guest in the house.

Rebecca saw Bhupen sitting in garden chair and sipping tea. Normally Bhupen never liked to be disturbed by anyone but Rebecca walked up to him and enquired, 'Good morning *Saab.* How is *Memsaab*?'

'She is fine Rebecca. See if the paperwala has brought the morning paper.' Bhupen did not want anyone around him. He wanted seclusion, so he deflected her away. In fact he was dreaming something to make improbable to probable. Once he finished his tea, he went inside and planned his morning. He went in the bath room, had a good wash and dressed up for the day. Joe had come with the morning papers.

Bhupen sat down at his working table and went through the latest happenings in the world. This was his daily routine. While he was browsing through the newspaper he felt as if someone was standing behind. He turned his neck. Sharabni was standing there with her uneven hair falling around her head. She was looking very cute.

'Oh! So you got up.'

'Yes Mr. Bhupen, Good morning.'

'Good morning. How are you feeling now?'

'I have some hang over, otherwise I am alright.'

'It will be over after some time.'

Bhupen called for Joe and asked him to give black coffee to Sharabni.

'I vaguely remember that I created some raucous last evening. I really apologise for all my silly behaviour.'

'There was nothing as such.'

Bhupen was discreet about his feelings for her, whereas she was quite vocal. She said, 'I wish I could have fallen in love with a person like you rather than Ajit.'

Joe came and placed the coffee tray on the table next to Sharabni. 'Forget about every thing. Have your coffee and relax.'

'How about you?'

'I just finished my tea.'

Sharabni sipped the coffee while Bhupen went through the paper. He marked the important news. After coffee, Sharabni went into the bathroom and had a good wash. But she had a problem what to wear as her clothes reeked. She came out in Bhupen's night suit and asked him, 'How can I go to my house in such dress.'

'Today you are on holiday. You need not to go anywhere. After sometime you will have breakfast. Now you just relax.'

'But I have to go for my work.'

'What time do you to go?'

'Dot at nine.'

Bhupen strained his brain. He looked at the picture of Deepti which was put on the wall next to his computer. It reminded him of the saris, which he had bought for her and were lying in his cupboard for years. He went into his bedroom opened the cupboard and took out a packet.

'Sharabni here are some saris. You may choose any one to wear now.' She unpacked the bundle and picked up a Sanganeri print. But the matching blouse was unstitched.

'Mr. Bhupen, still the problem exists. There is no blouse.'

Bhupen yelled for Joe who was fixing breakfast.

'Yes sir.'

'Ask your wife to bring some blouse matching this sari.'

Joe rushed to his room and brought several blouses. Sharabni chose one and dressed up. The blouse was loose but in such situation it served the purpose. Bhupen gave Sharabni's clothes to Joe and instructed him to get them washed. Sharabni was off after the breakfast.

All the time in the morning Bhupen pretended to be poised, but he was not. Rather since last night he was delirious. After decades he was swept away with the loving feeling for a woman. In fact, it was his dire physical and mental requisition to have a woman of his choice. Ever since he learnt that Deepti was married and had grown up children, such feelings were lying dead deep in his unconsciousness and he had reconciled with the existing way of life. Of course he screwed several women but had no loving feeling for them. He thought that he might feel normal if he got to his work, therefore he decided to go the Studio. In the office, he found a letter for his immediate attention. Priyanka Roy had urged him to send her the matter for the brochure of the forth coming exhibition of his paintings. For a while he forgot his anxiety and called Priyanka on his cell.

'Hello, Priyanka, It is convenient for me to email the material for publication. Is this modus operandi alright with you?'

'Perfectly alright.'

'So, you may have it shortly.'

He opened the computer, browsed for her email and attached the file of the material for publication and clicked the send box. Mail was sent successfully. He shut up the computer and went into the studio. He had stacked the paintings for the forth coming exhibition in one corner. He picked up an empty canvas placed it at the easel and sat in front of it. He tried to recollect the face of Sharabni in his mental screen, but it was blurred with the fainted image of Deepti. It was a peculiar psychological confusion in his mind. More he concentrated on Sharabni's face more prominent Deepti's image appeared in his imagination. Confusion. He left the idea to create a painting and decided to go to his house.

After lunch he drove to Arc Art gallery at Habitat Centre in Delhi. He discussed all the details of the contract regarding his exhibition in Delhi and then in Paris with Priyanka. He made it clear to her that he would visit Paris only if she would pay for his passage and the stay in some reasonable good hotel. She did not commit straightway but bought time to think over to concede his offer.

After visiting a few friends at the Lalit Kala Studios at Rabindra Nagar, he shot back home. On the way to Gurgaon he bought a dozen of bottles of Whisky some Vodka and beer from a wine shop at Ansal Plaza. He intended to throw a cocktail party a day before the opening of the exhibition. Bhupen was crazy about throwing cocktail parties every now and then. This made him popular among the artists and art critics of the town. Though he was not a frolic kind of specie, but he enjoyed serious interaction with intellectuals. He never celebrated Holi festival but invited his coterie for New Eve celebrations.

When he reached home, he saw Sharabni sitting in the verandah. He parked the car in the garage. Sharabni walked towards the garage and confronted Bhupen who had just come out from the garage.

'Good Evening Mr. Roy.'

'Good Evening Sharabni. It is my pleasure to see you.'

'How was your day?'

'It was not bad. Well washing and cleaning muck of others' children is horrible. But I am paid for it. So I have no regrets.'

'Well, work is work. It may be big or small. Besides payment, you may learn the psychology of children, which you may use as research work for your higher education at some stage in life.'

'That is very true, but my contention was not to despise the nature of work. In fact when I handle the children at the creche, it reminds me all the time of my own child Kunal, who Mrs. Mondol has grabbed unethically. Mr. Roy I am a mother.'

'It is true. But I had no intention to hurt your feeling. I said it in a philosophical vein.'

'I do understand you Mr. Roy. I just met you for over 24 hours by now, but I feel as if I know you since ages. You are a noble soul.'

'No Sharabni I am as rakehell a man as any other one.' And he laughed.

'I wish you could be wicked with me. I have no hesitation in saying that you are love.'

'Will you join me for drink?' asked Bhupen.

'Not today. I was a big nuisance for you last night. Besides, I will have to go to my place today.'

'There is an assuaging way of drinking. If you go slow and take snacks off and on you can hold the drinks.'

Bhupen fixed a large whisky for himself and asked Joe to prepare some French fingers. He offered apple juice to Sharabni. He really wanted her to be drunk. But certainly he did not force her for it.

'Well Sharabni, you know very little about me.'

'But what all I have experienced is that you combine equipoise with tenderness in your person.'

'To be honest, I live in bad faith.'

'This confession itself reveals your living in good faith.'

'You try to be logician, but you are not. You are very impulsive.'

'Mr. Roy I changed my mind. May I have a small whisky with soda?'

'You may have. But be very slow.'

'All right.'

Yester evening Sharabni had come to express her sincere gratitude to Bhupen, but today she had came with different intention. She was seeking a perspective suitable man to live in with Bhupen. How far she would be succeeding in her design, she was not sure as yet. She pretended that she would like to go to her place, but in reality she wanted to stay at his place. She had realized that she could not be fast with this seasoned man, otherwise she might lose him. When Bhupen gave her the drink, she took it but instead of sipping it she kept it on the table. She was capricious.

'Mr. Roy I give a second thought to my temptation to drinks. Thank you for the drink, but I will stick to apple juice.'

Bhupen was in a fix. He could not understand her capricious state of mind, however he said, 'Do not drink if you don't want. Decision is yours.'

'Thank you for everything you did for me. I will be off for my house.' said Sharabni after taking the apple juice.

'How will you go?'

'By rickshaw.'

'Alright.'

Bhupen called for Joe and asked him to get a peddle rickshaw for Sharabni from the rickshaw stand. When Joe brought the rickshaw, Bhupen came till gate to see her off. He stood on the gate till she was out of sight. He grunted and came inside to his drink's table.

Sharabni did not turn up for several weeks. It was one Sunday evening some time in mid October, when friends poured in his house for the cocktail party. Joe and Rebecca had made the arrangement for the gathering in the backyard lawn. Priyanka was among the early birds. She was accompanied by Sharabni. Bhupen was surprised to see Sharabni. He retrieved his amorous feeling for Sharabni, which had extinguished by then. He had practically washed her out from his mind. When Priyanka was introducing Sharabni to Bhupen she said that they knew each other very well.

Bhupen, queried, 'Priyanka how do you know Sharabni?'

'I met her on Durga Puja festival in Sushant Lok. She is terrific at Tagore Sangeet.'

'Oh really? This I didn't know. I witnessed some other kind of music with her.' He laughed and looked at Sharabni, who felt embarrassed at his remarks. But she shot back.

'Priyanka, what sort of an artist he is, he does not respond to beautiful girl. He tortures them with his silence and luke-warm response.'

'Mr. Roy, what are these quizzical words from Sharabni.'

'She is your friend. You may comprehend better than I could do… Please excuse me.' He said to the young women and dashed to an old friend, who had just arrived.

'Hello Amlendu! It is indeed a pleasure to have you. Let's sit in that corner where I have displayed "Nude in Blue" on an easel.'

They sat down with drinks in their hand and got engrossed in serious conversation. Some more art critics including Krishnan joined them.

By nine o'clock the lawn was fully crowded with guests. There was excessive hubbub in the lawn, people were revelling with drink in their hands. Some youngsters were clinging to their girl friends. Sharabni did not restrain and relishing French Red wine. When she was slightly tipsy, she dashed to Bhupen and implanted a long kiss passionately on his cheek. Amlendu and Krishnan — a seasoned art critics were reviewing his blue nude in cubism on an easel next to them. Krishnan pierced his gaze at Sharabni and commented, 'Is she the kill for your blue nude? But she is brown. Good material for bed.'

Bhupen laughed and said, 'Dirty old man you always think of lust not of love or sublimation.'

'Sublimation is just self denial. Eat drink and be merry.'

Amlendu interrupted the conversation and asked Bhupen to move inside as they can not talk about his new creations in such confusing hubbub. But Krishnan insisted upon to stay back in the lawn. 'Inside we will miss the sight of the beautiful women. You both are dry old crows,' protested Krishnan.

'You may stick to your seat in the garden, we are going inside,' Amlendu proclaimed.

Bhupen and Amlendu receded inside the living room, where Joe had arranged everything at the bar as an alternative for special guests. Bhupen had displayed some of his interesting paintings in cubism in the living room. Amlendu lipped his drink and looked at the fantastic canvases.

'Beautiful! It is marvellous work. I will review this exhibition for *The Times.* Have you heard from Deepti?'

'Amlendu she is forgotten episode.'

While they were engrossed in serious matters, Sharabni staggered in with drink in her hand. She was followed by Krishnan.

All the four clustered around the bar table. Bhupen introduced Sharabni to Amlendu with the remarks, 'Amlendu this young woman is an unusually intelligent scholar and had worked on Jean Paul Sartre, but she does not have access to press for her work.'

'Did you graduate in philosophy?' asked Amlendu.

'No I had had English as major discipline, but circumstances tracked me on Sartre. Existence for some unlucky women is Challenge.'

'You talk sense. I think you are a victim of some misogynist.'

'Yes, your guess is correct.'

Amlendu asked Bhupen, 'Give me the photographs and the brochure of your paintings. *The Time* has already set aside two pages space for a feature on you and your latest paintings.' Bhupen gave him the photographs and all relevant papers for his article. Soon after Amlendu was off for his office as he had to send an urgent story for *The London Times*. Krishnan looked at Bhupen. 'Why do you act as an escapist? You have invited people and now hiding yourself like a rat in a hole. Please join your guests outside.'

'Krishnan it was an urgent business with Amlendu. It is over. Let's go out.'

They moved out on the lawn. Bhupen looked at Sharabni and announced, 'Ladies and gentlemen Sharabni will entertain you with Tagore Sangeet. Three claps for Sharabni.'

Sharabni was taken aback to hear the unexpected announcement. She took some time to restore composure. She recited a few poems from *Geetanjli* in her melodious voice. She spellbound the revellers. Bhupen did not know that she was an excellent singer — better than the professional singers. For him it was a new discovery. One after the other, she presented seven songs.

By twelve o'clock all guests except Sharabni dispersed. Joe with the help of hired squad of workers cleared up the paraphernalia and went away with Rebeeca to his room. Sharabni and Bhupen were left alone. Though she was tipsy but did not create any nuisance the way she did during her last visit. But she gestured through body language to share bed with Bhupen. But he was not yet prepared to face the consequences. Sharabni switched off all the lights of the house and dragged Bhupen on the bed to indulge in physical rapture. Bhupen did not resist. He held her with his arms round his body. Sharabni voluntarily undressed. So did Bhupen. Their legs intertwined with their thigh on thigh. Both relished the orgy.

Sharabni got up early morning and looked at the naked body of Bhupen. She covered him with a cotton sheet and went into bath room. The sound of gurgling of the tap water woke up Bhupen. He realized what all had happened at night and quickly dressed up. Sharabni came out and said. 'Good Morning Bhupen.'

'What Good Morning? You seduced me at night.'

'Do you regret it?'

'No.'

'Nor do I regret.'

'Will you marry me?'

'Soon after my divorce case is settled.'

'Do you know that I had been sharing bed with other women?'

'That was your physical need. None of those women loved you, so I do not mind. In fact I love you.'

'Sharabni I do confess that I too love you. Ever since I saw you getting drunk last time, I developed very tender feelings for you.'

'That I knew.'

They had wash and before Joe could come they were dressed up properly for their day's work.

Bhupen engaged the best lawyer of the country and the divorce case was settled in a year's time. Soon after getting the copy of the judgment they applied for court marriage. After a moth the marriage took place in a court. Amlendu, Krishnan, and Priyanka acted as witnesses.

Mukta

Once Ajeet Prasad Panwar was promoted as Assistant Engineer and transferred from Balgarh to Delhi, his only daughter Mukta faced difficulties to adjust to the new environment, new school, new friends, and new neighbourhood. In Balgarh, she was studying in a small government school. Thinking that, it would be better for Mukta to join some public school; so with words from his boss to a principal, he secured admission for her in a public school. Though, at school she could not adjust but at home she tried to explore all possible avenues to quench her inquisitions. Unlike other urban children, she had not yet developed the status complex as being the daughter of a senior official and played with the children of the servants. Climbing trees, running after birds, playing with the pups of a street bitch which had delivered five or six of them a week ago. Her father was a stern disciplinarian. When he found her tramping wildly in street or playing with drop out children of the servants, he would not bombard her directly. He would immediately call his wife Parvati with ferocious look and tell her to cultivate decent manners in their daughter. Mukta did not pay a heed to anyone's command. She was growing obstinate and carefree. She would not give hand to her mother in kitchen or would carry tray for entertaining the repulsive visitors. She would come from the school, leave her satchel on the dirty old table with indelible circles of dirty glasses that father had bought before she was flushed out in the world from her mother womb. Her clothes were always dirty. She whistled at the morose herd of uncle and aunts.

Mukta was growing as a complex girl. At school, she defied her teachers in different ways. She was often late as she had to travel by public transport standing between the heavily packed crowds. When teacher asked her why she was late, frowningly she would reply, 'Mam you ask the transport department why the bus are running late or my father to buy a car to drop me at the school in the fashion the other students come. Do you understand my problem? Please don't pop your eyes. You can not scare me.'

Oppressed at home and at school, Mukta did not compromise with her situation and was turning into an ambitious girl. Though she had been at English school, and her classmates laughed at her pronunciation, but she did not give up her determination to beat out her competitors in their own game. She was intelligent otherwise. She was fast at picking up English language and in a years time she was ahead of other girls not only in English but in other subjects too. Though she still faced difficulties in speaking English but her writings were far advanced for her age.

When she grew into adolescent, she ceased to play with the servants' children. The innocence had extinguished with the passage of time. She reacted to charming vicious bloody sexy rich girls, who despised her and refused to accept her in their fold. She was lonely at school and lonely at home. She pretended as if she cared damn for them. She isolated herself and turned to books. She developed keen interest in literature and found a way out for her loneliness. Mr. Ajeet Prasad had maintained a good collection of literary books. He sensed a new change in Mukta. He hardly had any communication with her and if he had to convey anything to Mukta it was through his wife Parvati. But once he found her plunged into Dickens or Jane Austin in her tiny room, he tried to converse on literary personalities like Shakespeare, Bernard Shaw and many more. But these were very brief moments. Because, she was not very fond of him so she was grumpy on such occasions.

Her mother? She was from a rich but conservative Rajput clan with *pati parmeshwar* culture in her feminine veins. She was not a very highly educated woman but could maintain social norms with her middle class relatives. Her religious rituals looked quite idiotic to Mukta. On one Sunday she tried to persuade Mukta to go to temple with her but she would out rightly reject her persuasion and asked, 'Ma! Why do you go to temple and worship that cylindrical round headed stone?'

'You atheist, God will never be kind to you if you speak like this.'

'You mean that stone will curse me,' Mukta laughed hysterically.

'Have you gone insane?'

'Not me. You might have gone.'

'You speak like this to your mother? *Hi Ram* what is wrong with the girl' she cried and went away in the kitchen.

Mukta had no intention to hurt her mother but she was so raged by her loneliness that she took out all her frustration on her mother. For how long she could keep herself occupied with the reading of book or the home task assigned by the teacher. Beside, she was grown up and the influence of pop culture on her mind had made her characteristically a rebellion girl.

She went well with a girl who was far more rebellious and defied all norms of the permissive society. It was Helen. She boasted about herself, 'I am Helen of Troy.' Mukta was rebellious alright but she had different cause for it than that of Helen. She was victim of social disparity which she expressed through her intransigence; whereas Helen was nymphomaniac and for her sexual kicks she defied the school authority. The peculiarity of her body language imprinted curiosity in Mukta's mind. She often carried playboy magazines and nude photographs. They bunked the school and spent time in park viewing the nude pictures. Some time they would go to school loo and smoke cigarettes. Helen's brother Robert was a gay and always surrounded by sexy boys. One of them was Bhadur Singh (Bhalu to his friends).

Mukta's impudence was increasing more and more. She had some understanding with her mother, but due to her fascination for nude photographs and unwelcome hot argument on the existence of God she was now cut off from her mother too. Now she lived an extreme secluded life at home. Unfortunately she was the only child of her parents. She was sorry for this.

One day Helen dropped in her house. She confronted Mukta's mother.

'Hi old woman! Is Mukta there? I have just come to see her.'

Hearing the peculiar words Mr. Ajeet Prasad walked out from his room where he was scrutinizing the official files. Helen looked at him and stretching forward her hand for shaking, she said, 'I am Helen — Mukta's friend I have come to see her.' Both Mr. and Mrs. Prasad were so embarrassed to see this tartly girl that they did not speak anything to her, but they were boiling from within. Of course they did not reveal their furiousness. Ensemble Mukta walked out of her room and saw Helen standing in the living room. She told her parents that Helen was her classmate and escorted her to her room. Helen was shocked to see Mukta's little dingy room.

After looking around at the smoky drab walls, dirty furniture and a small bed with a shabby mattress she mouthed, 'How can you live in such a shabby place? My Dog Tim has bigger room than yours and very neat and clean.'

Mukta had no answer to her comment, but certainly she did mind her remarks and realized within that this woman was a big show off. When she went away, her mother came and asked her, 'Who was this shameless girl? Why did she come? Do not invite her again. She does not look to be from a dignified family.'

'Ma, I did not invite her. She came of her own.'

'Tell her when you meet her that she is not welcome here. Is it clear to you?'

Mukta got more exasperated, 'Why the hell you are after my life. Why have you not killed me when you threw me out of you?'

Parvati was stunned as if struck by lightning. She felt as if the earth was slipping away from under her feet. She did not expect such a shot from her daughter. She snorted in disgust and disappeared into her bedroom.

Mukta realized her incondite expression and felt that she had damaged the dignity of motherhood. She regretted for what all she had said. She went over to her mother and touching her feet, apologized for her misbehaviour. Her mother howled and tears were flooding from her eyes. She clamped Mukta. Then onward the mother and daughter were careful not to defy each other. However Mukta kept her state of seclusion. She hardly had any communication with her mother except for the basic requisition, food, clothes or at the most for extra money for her basic need.

Mukta restrained her desires to indulge in seeing porno magazines, because she wanted to avoid Helen, but Helen often glued to her. One day when Mukta was on the way to home and was standing at the bus stop, Helen bumped into her. Bhalu was with him. They had planned to play bull and cow in the secluded old monument in a park. Helen introduced Bhalu to Mutka. Bhalu remarked, 'Hi chick, why don't you join us? You are a good kill.'

'What do you mean by a good kill?' asked Mukta

'A good thing to fuck.'

Mukta looked down and took out one of her sandal which had nails of practically all the shoe menders nearby her house. She held it firmly in her hand and gave a good bang at his face. He was bleeding. Before he realized that he was bleeding Mukta jumped in to the bus which incidentally arrived. She could see from the window that the people were having a good laugh at the happening.

Since then a change took place in Mukta's mental make up. She stopped pinching money from her mother's box, she stopped smoking and kicked Helen as and when she tried to lure her into sexual trips. Her self confidence was getting stronger.

Once she passed out from the school and joined St. Mary College, she participated in the extra curricular activities. She wanted to out do the other counterparts from rich families and to some extent she achieved her target. She showed tremendous will power at play ground. She was good at literature. Luckily she had read many of the books that were prescribed for her courses during school days. Now it paid her good dividends. She was far ahead than other students in her studies. She had become very thrifty. She would sit in the library for hours together for her studies. She participated in dramatics.

On the annual function of the college, Mukta participated in a full length play Othello by Shakespeare. She carried out the role of Desdemona superbly. The elite of the town including fashion designers, artists, bureaucrats and politicians thronged the hall to see the play. All praised Mukta for her superb performance. She was famous over night.

Next day the college closed for a special holiday. On the first opening day a young lady Ritu Berry barged into the office of the Principal of St. Mary College and requested her to fix her meeting with Mukta. The Principal asked her to wait in the visitors' room and sent a word for Mukta that a woman has come to see her, so she might see her in the visitors' room as and when she was free from her class. Mukta was attending her English lecture, so after the lecture she went to meet the unknown visitor.

When she entered into the visitors' room a woman got up and said with a smile on her face, 'Mukta, I am Ritu — Ritu Berry. I must congratulate you for your brilliant performance in Othello.'

'Thank you so much Ritu.'

'You know after seeing your talent and potential for acting, I have come to offer a very lucrative position. You may join our organization. We make serials for T.V.'

'But I have yet to complete my graduation.'

'You will be paid much more than a graduate is paid.'

'That is not the point. I want to pursue my education.'

'Then you may work for us as freelance actor.'

'Give me some time to think.'

'Here is my card. Please let me know about your decision at the earliest possible instance. Yes Mukta, it is an opportunity for you to catch Fortune from its forelocks. Once it leaves you, you won't be able to catch it as it balds from behind. Strike when the iron is red. Do you have contact number?'

'Yes I do have.'

'Please give.'

Ritu took her phone number and was off with enforcing her plea. 'Mukta please do think over of my proposal seriously.'

Mukta was in double mind. While she was excited about the offer of a break through, she was hesitant to accept it at the cost of her studies. She went home and pondered on Ritu's offer. She certainly had been craving for such opportunity, but when it came in she was puzzled whether to avail it or not.

It was Sunday. Mukta had been tossing in bed as she had slept very late. Ritu telephoned her. Her mother Parvati picked up the telephoned. *'Kaun bolti hai?'* (Who is speaking?)

'I am Ritu and want to speak to Mukta.'

'Just hold on. I will call her.'

Parvati came to Mukta's room and told her about a phone call. She got up and sluggishly staggered to telephone.

'Hello! Mukta is on line.'

'Hello Mukta, what are you doing this evening?'

'Nothing very special.'

'See there is a party to celebrate the opening of an exhibition of paintings by Hussain at India Habitat Centre. I think you must come.'

'But I do not know anyone. Besides I have not been invited as such.'

'You come with me. I will come to pick you up. Be ready by seven.'

'All right.'

Mukta gave her consent, but she was nervous. She had never been to such a celebration. Besides, she had nothing very special to wear. She strained her mind and thought of some thing interesting. She had seen some women artists wearing tribal dresses from Gujarat in some T.V. show. She had bought some thing very fancy from Ahmedabad when she had gone on an educational trip with other college girls. She dressed up in this fancy suit and waited for Ritu. Around seven thirty Ritu honked in front of her house. She came out and sat down next to Ritu in her car. Mukta was feeling relieved that Ritu did not come inside. She would have been embarrassed to have her in her shabby house.

It was a cocktail party sponsored by a liquor tycoon on the occasion of the opening of the exhibition. People were trooping in a big way. Ritu introduced Mukta to many well-known actors and artists. Surprisingly people were fascinated by Mukta. She was looking nifty in embroidered maroon long *ghagra* with matching *choli* with round small mirror embedded in between the embroidery work. While she was going round to see the paintings, the young artists were gluing to her. Ritu was grinning at her situation, but Mukta was developing claustrophobia. Ritu asked her to have a glass of wine instead of apple juice. She refused at the first instance, but she gave second thought to Ritu's suggestion and had a small whisky. After a few sips, her nervousness was gone. She was a different Mukta a self confident Mukta. This was her first experience of a cocktail party. She realized that most of people had come just to socialize and to revel after taking a couple of drinks. Very few had come to see the paintings. She liked oil on canvas with a woman in blue with pathetic expression on her face surrounded by hideous looking man. While she was looking at this painting, Ritu was observing her with attentive look at her face.

'Mukta you like this paintings.'

'I appreciate it for its expressive quality. Don't you think it expresses the oppression of women?'

'Yes, that's right? Mukta are you a human right activist?'

'Not exactly, but I certainly read fiction on such themes. You see...' A young man came and talked to Ritu. 'Hello Ritu. Who is this young grace?'

'Krishan she is my friend Mukta.'

'Hi Mukta! I saw you observing painting very seriously. Are you a painter or an art student?'

'No I am just a student of English literature.'

Ritu interrupted, 'Krishan she is an actress — a powerful actress. Only thing she is missing the proper exposure.'

'Wow. It is nice to hear.'

Mukta was feeling odd to hear comments on her. She fumbled, 'Ritu lets go now.'

'Hold on dear. Are you getting bored?'

'No, that's not the point.'

'Then what's it? Have another drink. And talk to Krishan. He promotes young talents.'

They had refills and walked out of the crowd and drifted away from palm court and sat down on stairs. Ritu and Krishan discussed their future plans about a new serial on the story of the murder of a woman Journalist. Mukta might act as the journalist.

It was 11 o'clock when they left Habitat Centre. Ritu offered Mukta spending the night with her at her place, but in the morning she had to go to the college, so she asked her to drop her at her place. Ritu reached Mukta's place, stopped the car, walked out and affectionately planted a kiss on her right cheek (friendship kiss) and drove away to her house.

When Mukta knocked at the door her mother opened the door and squealed, 'Where were you at this hour?'

'Ma I have gone with a friend. I am grown up enough to take care of myself.'

'Shut up. The grown up girl of a decent families does not ramble late at night.'

Mukta flurried, 'Why don't you let me live life in peace?'

She looked at her mother scornfully and went in to her room. She changed her apparel, opened back side window and crashed on the bed.

One day, Mukta had gone to St. Stephen College for a declamation contest. After the function she met a young man at long tea. He walked up to Mukta and said, 'Mukta, you know I met you at Habitat Centre. You looked so fashionable there I had to strain my memory chamber to identify you. You look so simple in white *salwar kameez*.'

'What do you do?' asked Mukta.

'I am Kartik and a student of literature in final year in this college.'

'It is nice to meet you Kartik. I think we may be like minded,' said Mukta

The day Mukta passed out with simple first division in English honour from Delhi University; she visited Ritu and disclosed the new of becoming a graduate. Ritu was very happy. She treated her with French wine and cheese cubes. With a little curiosity, Mukta asked, 'Where is your hubby?'

'He is a fiend and may be tripping on brown sugar with his lousy friends.'

'What does he do otherwise?'

'He does nothing.'

'Where does he get money from to buy drugs?'

'I give him money for his drugs. If I do not give him he beats me.'

'Do you share bed with him?'

'Where should I go for my sex release?'

'I really feel sorry for you. Why don't you divorce him and get married to some sane person like Krishan.'

Ritu had tears in her eyes. She wiped her face with a tissue paper lying on the table and said, 'Mukta I do not loathe this man. I still love him. He is a victim of circumstances. Ours was the love marriage. Can you imagine he discarded his multimillionaire parents for me and walked out for me from his house? He was a prominent journalist in a reputed daily. Who did not know Keshava? But his father Vijay Prakash managed to get him thrown out of the organization thinking that he would return to him.'

'Looks like a filmy story.'

'It is a reality.'

For a while silence prevailed between them. When Mukta wanted to leave, Ritu drove her to her house. That night she did not sleep and brooded over Ritu's plight. From next day she joined Ritu as full time actor to act in her serials. After shooting, Mukta some time moved with Kartik but mostly she accompanied Ritu to some party or the other. Financially she was now independent. Her parents did not object Kartik's visit to their house, rather imagined perspective son in law in him, but he was without a job. So they were waiting for him to get some suitable position. Ritu frequented her house in the morning and lifted Mukta for the work. Apart from acting Mukta helped Ritu in brushing off her scripts. They were now very intimate friends.

It was the third week of July. The weather was quite humid. Ritu came to lift Mukta for shooting an episode of a new serial. They reached the studio and found that there was electricity failure and the generator set was under repairs. So they escaped in the open space under a shady tree and chattered about their personal matter. Mukta asked Ritu if she could find some work for Kartik.

She immediately said that she needed a hand for handling the property. So after a week Kartik also joined Ritu.

When Ajeet Prasad and Parvati came to know that Kartik has got a placement, they went over to see his parents and proposed the marriage between Kartik and Mukta. Kartik was all out to marry Mukta, but when her mother declared the decision about her marriage to Kartik, She flared up and squealed, 'You could have asked me before going over their house. Kartik is just a friend he is not husband material for me. Please never talk to me on this issue in future.'

Father never had hold on Mukta. Even mother was losing it. There was hardly any communication between Mukta and her parents now. Only person she cared for was Ritu. But for the last one week she was not coming to studio. Except Kartik she had no other close boy friend. She spent most of her time with him in the studio looking after the daily routine.

Mukta was anxious about Ritu. She telephoned her and found that Keshava was in hospital on the verge of death.

Next day it was 15 August and Mukta was glued to T.V. just to hear the Prime Minister's speech. The telephone rang Mukta brought down the volume of the T.V. and picked up the receiver.

'Mukta on line.'

'Mukta it is Ritu. You know Kashava is no more. He died an hour ago.'

'Good for him and good for you.'

'What a stone hearted person you are!'

'Ritu you must understand he was dead long ago when his father got him out of the job. Physically he was alive, but mentally he was dead. Any way in a short while I will be with you.'

Keshava was cremated in Lodhi Cremation Ground. No one from his parent's family attended the last rites. Kartik performed the ignition ceremony. Even Ritu's parents did not turn up. Both Ritu and Keshava were rebellions. For a few days Mukta stayed with Ritu. At time when Ritu looked in blank, Mukta advised her, 'Ritu you have seen more autumns or springs than I had seen, but certainly autumn is followed by spring. I can understand that you loved a man and lost him but not to his parents but to death. So what is the regret?'

A month after the death of Keshava, Ritu went to Studio, Mukta had been handling the production so there was no financial loss, but many official works were pending. Court notices, planning securing further assignments all had to be tackled. She had very loyal team of workers. So in a short time every thing was regularized. Mukta had become a well know actor in the country. She was getting many offers to act on the big screen. But she did not want to leave Ritu in lurch especially when she needed her most to run the organization. But her father-in-law Vijay Prakash tried to harass Ritu. He used his contact in income tax department and got Ritu Studio raided. Nothing came out it, but for a month Ritu and Mukta remained occupied with unnecessary running around to fight the case in the court of law.

Ritu had launched a new venture — a movie 'Rebellious Girl' for the big screen. Mukta had done the script and she was playing the role of heroine. The project had been financed by a big Colonizer who was a rival of Vijay Prakash. When the shots of the last scene were taken, a gun man appeared on the scene. No one took notice of him. He shot two bullets at Ritu but Mukta was moving towards the hero as per requisition of the story, so accidentally she came in front of Ritu who was directing the Cameraman. The bullet went in her chest. And she collapsed on the floor. Kartik kept his wits and grabbed the gun man from behind. Police were called and he was handed over to police. Later on he confessed that he was hired by Vijay Prakash to murder Ritu. In the mean while Ritu rushed Mukta to hospital but she died before reaching hospital.

Adhunika

It was Sunday. Kokila was lazing in her bed when the telephone rang. She picked up the phone and was excited to know that Rajneesh — Rajneesh Patel was on the line.

'Rajneesh your call makes me crazy with wanton feelings in my mind.'

Rajneesh asked, 'What are you doing in the afternoon?'

'Well, what I will do here?'

'Then baby come to Lover's Den at Grand Hotel by one.'

'Certainly Love I will be there.'

Kokila saw her mother stepping in her bedroom, so she changed the conversation. 'So, Sulbha certainly we meet some time in the afternoon. Do you understand…' she closed the mobile and said to her mother. 'Mama you must learn manners. You should knock at the door before entering the room.'

'Do I have to take your permission to enter into your room?

'Yes Mama.'

'The breakfast is ready. Please come to the dinning table.'

'Please bring the breakfast here.'

Mandakani did not mind her daughter's symptomatic behaviour and went back into the kitchen. She fixed breakfast for her daughter and carried to her room. Kokila was in the bathroom. She put the tray on a table and went to her son's room.

'Mohit *bete* get up, table is laid with breakfast,' Mandakni said with affection.

'Mom let me relax. Don't disturb me. More you grow old more cynical you are getting. You are too much.' He pulled his quilt and went to sleep. He had been out in a disco bar for the night and had come in the morning at five o'clock.

Tall with sharp features, big eyes and wheatish complexion, Mandakni was a very beautiful. An affectionate mother and devoted wife, Mandakani never offended anyone including the servants. She did not mind if her husband or children speak rudely to her. Her husband Srikant was short tempered. She was not an illiterate woman; she had done her graduation from Agra University. She was not a fanatic but certainly believed in basic tenets of Indian culture. Naturally she had inherited it from her parents. She had been brought up in a well to do Kayasath family. Her father was an indologist and mother was a Principal of DAV Public School.

It was the month of January and her husband Srikant had invited half a dozen of his friends for lunch, so after preparing breakfast Mandakani plunged in the preparation of lunch. Though she had a maid to help her, but as per her habit she was cooking diligently every thing with her own hands. At about mid day Srikant's friends trooped in. Srikant had made the arrangement for lunch in the open space which was flooded with welcoming Sun. When Mandakni saw the guests pouring in, she immediately placed the bear bottles and the tray of ice cubes on the large table with marble top. She had already kept the bear tumblers there. She had prepared vegetable kababs and kept these in the microwave. Once his friends settled, she carried kababs in a big plate and placed next to the beer bottle, and went back to kitchen to attend her unfinished work.

Srikant went over the marble table and tried to open the beer bottle, but there was no opener so he yelled, 'Mandakani!'

'*Oji* what did you call me for?' Mandakani asked.

'Where is the bottle opener? Who will bring it? Your father?'

'Father is in Banaras, but I will bring it,' she said innocently.

His friends had a good laugh at Mandakani's answer. Srikant smiled. 'She is a fatuous woman.' One of the friends Mr. Shyam had come with his wife Purnima. Purnima did not like Srikant's behaviour with his wife but she did not express her disgust. However another young woman journalist from *The Hindustan Times* recited a quotation from Maithli Sharan Gupt's poem: *'Abla jiwan hai tumhari yehi kahani, Anchal me hai dhood aur ankh me pani.'* (Oh passive woman! Your story is sad. You have milk in your chest, but you have tears in our eyes.) Again there were peals of laughter.

Mandakni brought the bottle opener, gave it to Srikant and rushed back into the kitchen. More or less she had cooked every thing and had stored some in the micro oven; some she had kept on the burner with low flame. Some she had wrapped in heavy clothes and kept near the burner.

The guests were enjoying the bubbling bear with kababs. They talked about culture vulture, women liberation and the latest films. Mandakni served them warm food.

Before dispersing, one man commented, 'Your wife is as nifty as Madhuri Dikshit.'

'No! She is like Asha Parikh,' said another.

When Mandakni heard the comment, she was indignant. She could tolerate the absurd behaviour of her children and husband, but not of the outsiders. She came forward and said, 'Respectable guests I have my own identity I am Mandakni.'

'Mandakni, you are not only an excellent cook, but an efficient managing hand too. I admire how single handed you have entertained so many people and thank you for your good lunch.'

'You are welcome,' said Mandakni. .

Kokila had gone out without telling her parents where she was going. So did Mohit was planning to go to some dancing club. Srikant did not care what his children were involved in and Mandakni had no hold on them. Kokila came very late at night. Mandakni saw through a window that she came with a boy on motor cycle. When Kokila opened the door with a duplicate key which she had procured long ago from her mother's cupboard, she was confronted by her mother in corridor.

'From where are you coming at such late hour? Who was this boy?

Kokila popped her eyes and muttered indignantly and went straight into her room. Mandakni followed her.

'Why the hell you are after my life? He is my friend. Now you leave my room otherwise I will throw you out.' Mandakni was shocked to see her daughter in frenzy. She thought it would be better to leave and walked away in disgust.

Mandakni could not sleep after that and in the morning when Srikant got up she went to kitchen and fixed up the bed tea for Srikant. Placing the tray on the side table Mandakni said in soft but pensive voice, '*Oji* do you know that Kokila is drifting away in wrong direction?'

'Early morning do not create unpleasantness. What has she done to you?'

'Last night she came at one o'clock. A young lad dropped her and when I asked who that boy was, she misbehaved with me.'

'Mandakni you are an old timer. The time has changed. We live in modern age. Let the children do what they want. Now you go and do your household chores and let me get ready for my office.'

'You do not understand the gravity of the situation.'

Srikant flared up and bombarded her. 'You are an idiot. Just get out from the room and let me have my tea in peace.'

Mandakni walked out from bedroom and was puzzled at her husband's attitude. She went in the kitchen to prepare breakfast.

Mohit had come and slipped in his room. When Mandakani saw him she fixed tea and went into his room to give him tea. She did not speak and kept the cup on the side table. Mohit looked at her mother with guilt. But there was no communication between them. As a child he was very loving and affectionate boy but he had changed now.

Srikant yelled, 'Mandakni.' She was ironing his shirt. On hearing Srikant, she immediately rushed in the bedroom. He looked at her with contempt. 'Where is my towel, where are my clothes?' he asked.

'The towel is on your shoulder and the clothes are here on the chair.'

'Alright. Now you may buzz off.'

When Mandakni came back to iron stand she saw the hot iron had burnt the shirt.

She murmured. 'Good God! What have I done?'

After the bath when Srikant picked up the clothes he did not like the shirt and yelled, 'Mandakni I need my sky blue shirt.'

Mandakni timidly went to Srikant, and showed the burnt shirt 'Sorry this is not worth wearing.' Srikant frowned with anger and slapped her on the face. She screamed and sunk on the floor.

Since then Mandakni stopped taking keen interest in house hold chores. Her enthusiasm was dead. If Srikant asked for anything she refused to comply with his demand. She shifted to guest room. Though she carried on with the kitchen work but after cooking food she would recede in her room and would not bother who was eating and who was not eating. Srikant's room was in complete mess — absolutely disorganized. Mandakni was expecting Srikant to apologize for his obnoxious behaviour. Mandakni loved Srikant, but she knew that what to speak of love Srikant had no respect for her. When Srikant did not come forward to compromise with Mandakni, she decided to take up a job in a school which she had been offered many times before. After a week she shifted to a working women's hostel taking a few necessary things of daily use.

While she was leaving Srikant was furious. 'Where are you going?'

'I may go to hell or heaven what difference it makes to you?'

'You are my wife.'

'Legally I may be your wife, but morally you have lost your right on me and me on you.'

'You will regret.'

'I regret even now. What to speak of responding my love for you never valued my devotion to you.'

Mandakni's eyes were wet which she wiped quickly. She jumped into the taxi which had been loaded with her luggage. Once Mandakni left, the maid with whom Mandakni was very kind also left. Srikant was in difficulties. The entire house was in mess. A man who was a managing director in a multinational company in Gurgaon was utterly failure in managing his home. It was no home. Home had disintegrated with the exit of Mandakni. He had to get up in the morning to make his tea. The utensils in the kitchen were dirty.

A week after Mandakni had relinquished the house; Srikant discovered that Mohit has been expelled from College for nonpayment of dues. He had siphoned away the money on his girl friends in discos and bars. Lately he indulged in drugs and to procure money for it he committed petty crimes like chain snatching or stealing stereos from cars or doing shop lifting. One day while lifting a bag lying on the seat in a car at the parking lot of Janpath Hotel, he was caught red handed. The owner of the car was a senior press reporter. He handed over Mohit to police.

The police inspector of Parliament Street Police Station telephoned Srikant, 'Mr. Srikant we have arrested a young man Mohit in a theft case. He says he is your son. Please come to police station for his identification, so that we may proceed with legal procedure.' Srikant was terribly upset to hear the news of his son's arrest. He was already indignant due to Mandakni's desertion. He left his office immediately and reached the police station, where he found his son in the lock up. He engaged a lawyer to get Mohit released on bail. It consumed his more than three hours to get Mohit bailed out.

Kokila was now absolutely free do what she desired to do. After the college, she would go to disco with Rajneesh and then in the evening along with like minded boys and girls they headed for Rajneesh's farm house in Gurgaon where they spent night plunging into orgy till late in the morning. After drugging heavily they would never know who paired with whom. But Kokila never allowed any boy except Rajneesh to use her body. In the morning they would disperse for their house. Kokila some time spent days together with Rajneesh at his farm house. She came to her house only once in a while to pick up her apparels.

This morning when she came to her house she found that his father and brother were engaged in a brawl. When Srikant saw Kokila slipping in her room, he got up and for the first time he shouted at her. 'Where the hell you were fooling around?'

'I had been out with my boy friend. And now please tone down your voice.'

Srikant never expected such a shot back. His blood pressure curved up and he collapsed on the floor. Luckily Mandakni had come at that moment. She had read in the morning paper about the arrest of her son, and she could not restrain herself so came home. When she found Srikant on the floor, she called the driver, who was standing near the car to ferry Srikant to his office. She asked him to lift Srikant and take him to bed. While the driver was lifting him from the floor, Mandakni called for the family doctor Aman Tuli and apprised him about the urgency. There was commotion in the house.

Kokila telephoned Rajneesh, 'Hello Rajneesh there is big *tamasha* in the house so I will be late.'

When Mandakni heard her daughter talking to her boy friend, she rushed towards her and snatched the receiver. She shouted, 'Your father is sick in the bed and you are talking to your friend.

Whose telephone is this? Your boy friend pays for it? With whose money you had been fooling around?'

Kokila was shocked to see her mother in different colours. She had never seen her mother in such a temper. She always thought that she was a timid cow. She could not tolerate her mother's scolding, so she decided to leave the house. When her mother saw Kokila picking the bag and moving out, she snatched it.

'It had been provided you by your father so you cannot take it away.'

She looked at her mother with contempt and left the home in a fit. Mandakni turn to Srikant who had recovered from the bout of blood pressure. He looked at Mandakni with compassion.

'Forgive me for my stupidity; I am really your culprit for all that has gone wrong in the house. Promise me that you will not leave me again.'

'Forget about every thing and now rest. The doctor has advised that you need at least one day complete rest' said Mandakani.

Srikant went to sleep. Mandakni hurried to Working Women Hostel and brought her luggage not to leave her house again.

When Kokila reached Rajneesh's farm house, she told Rajneesh that she had quitted the house for ever for him,

'Baby you are a fool. How will you support your self? Sharing bed is alright. If it gives me pleasure, you also enjoy. Am I wrong?'

Kokila said, 'Rajneesh don't joke. I'm serious.'

'I'm not joking I am apprising you of reality.'

Kolila was stunned. She could not believe that Rajneesh would behave like this.

Rajneesh, 'You often iteratively said that you love me?'

'But I never said I will accept you as my keep. If you like to have fun then bed is ready.'

'Hell with you. Do you think that I will surrender to you for your lust? I have no regret what all I had been doing. I accept my experience as my experience.'

She went straight to her school and requested to her friends to give her the notes of the last one week so that she could make up what she had missed in her studies. Then she came home. She apologized to her mother for her stupidity. Her mother was a very wise person. She welcomed her back home with love and affection. She was so moved by her mother's affectionate behaviour that she put her head on her shoulder and burst out with sob. Mandakni cooled her down and asked her to forget the past. After that Kokila never cried.

Kokila was a changed person. She had developed self confidence and very strong will power. People go to Yoga Centre or Great Guru to culminate their energy and will power, but God knows how she had become such an energetic woman. She developed clarity of thoughts to achieve some thing in life. She helped her mother in house hold chores and when she was free. She worked hard for her studies and passed her examination with distinction. Even her brother Mohit, who had been convicted for three months' jail, was released after a month for his gentlemanly behaviour. He joined his college. In the evening Mandakni helped her children in their studies.

In the mean while Kokila realised that she was pregnant. Many of her friends advised her to get it cleaned. But she refused to accept their advice, and resolved to bring out the fetus in the world. When her mother found that Kokila was having a child in her womb, she was very upset, but she did not rebuke Kokila, rather tried to find a way out to the serious problem.

'Child if you tell me who the man is, I may possible persuade him to marry you.'

'Please Mama, forget about such plan. Let me bring out this child in the world. And if you think it will be a stigma on the family, I will live away from family. Possibly I shall take up some work or the other and bring up the child.'

'No, Kokila, it is not the matter. Whose name the child will be registered in? The system demands the father's name.'

'Then the system will be changed and children shall be registered in mother's name too.'

Kokila was trying hard to find a suitable job without the help of father and mother. Luckily one day she was called for an interview by a software organization. The managing director Ms. Kanishta who knew Kokila well was so much impressed by Kokila that she was asked to join with immediate effect. She worked diligently in the organization and not only she earned the confidence of Kanishta but became a good friend also. The delivery time was near so Kokila applied for one month's leave which was sanctioned without any problem. She gave birth to a healthy baby girl. She named her Adhunika. Mandakani looked after Kokila during her delivery time. She was on her legs after a few days of the delivery. Kanishta came to see Kokila in the hospital and gave her moral support. When Kokila joined her duty after a few weeks of the delivery, Mandakni looked after the small baby girl at home.

But a new problem had crept up. The women in neighbourhood gossiped about Kokila for giving birth without being married. Mouth to mouth publicity was so brisk that the entire colony made fun of Srikant's family. It did not affect Kokila. She had become a strong stoic character, but Mandakni was quite upset. When ever she went out to buy daily needs, or stood out on the terrace to spread the slushy clothes, women from neighbourhood squinted from their windows and jerked their shoulders with contempt.

Being sick of the taunts and contempt of the neighbours, Mandakani suggested to Srikant to dispose off the house and to buy a new one in some unknown colony. When Kokila came to know that her parents are planning to buy a new house. She was quite upset. Naturally her parents were facing social stigma because of her. She wanted to stay away from her parents, but they refused to let her go. She devised a way out and took Kanishta into confidence and explaining her odd situation she requested her to transfer her to England. Kanishta was very understanding and managed in a week's time to transfer her to London office.

Kokila took the little Adhunika and a maid and flew away to London. Her parents came to see her off at airport. Her mother was so sentimental about the departing of Kokila and Adhunika that she broke down with tears in her eyes. But she immediately regained her equanimity and gave a parting kiss to both Kokila and Adhunika.

Once she settled properly, Kokila devoted her evenings inking her own story and the destitution of Indian women. Sometimes she would introspect and analysed her short coming. She contemplated on her mother's characteristics and found that she was a woman with difference. Some times she thought of the future of Adhunika. She was living for this girl and wanted Adhunika to achieve what she could not have.

Every body in the family was concerned about Adhunika. Grand father grand mother often wrote and some time telephoned to find out about her welfare. Now she was grown up and could talk to her grannies. Some times Mohit also e-mailed from States. After passing out from Harvard University, he had taken up a position with Hewllet-Packard.

After passing out of the school Adhunika joined Oxford University. Now Kokila had enough time to complete her book. During Charismas holidays, Kokila invited her mother and father. Srikant had been frequenting London but her mother's was first visit. She was ecstatic to see Adhunika grown up as beautiful lass. She had seen her last when she was just an infant of four or five month. She conversed with her grand mama in Hindi fluently. After a week both Srikant and Mandakni flew back to India. Before they left for India, Kokila told her parents that once Adhunika secured her graduation, she might come to India for the release of her book which she might finish by then.

It was July 2000. Adhunika passed her post graduation in Sociology and immediately after that she got Four Foundation Fellowship. Kokila had finished her book and gave it to Light of

East Publishers for publication. She decided to get it released in September on the 21st birthday of Adunika.

On 30th September the Resident Director of Light of East Publisher organized the release of the book '*My Story*' at the Mayur Community Club. Very selective people were invited. Kokila was sitting with Adhunika and her parents. She got up and went to mike and gave a brief account of the genesis of the book and said specifically that it was dedicated to her daughter Adhunika. After the release of the book, one journalist asked Kokila, 'Madam! Will you tell the name of the father of your daughter?'

A man with unkempt beard with mixture of black and white hair dressed in *kurta pajama*, (he had read about the release of the book in morning paper) had come uninvited got up.

'I am the father.'

He staggered forward and gave some papers to Adhunika and receded back to walk away from the site. Kokila looked at the paper which the mysterious man had given to Adhunika. It was the deed of the transfer of his farm house in the name of Adhunika. Kokila said in a melodramatic voice, 'Mama once you asked me who the boy was? This man was that boy.'

Mandakni said, 'Kokila call him back.'

'Mama I really can't call him. Yes if Adhunika wants to call him, it is her decision.'

Adhunika cried, 'Papa! Papa! Come back.'

Rajneesh turned back and looked at Adhunika with pathetic smile, but he was hesitant to move forward. 'I have committed unpardonable sin my child,' said in a pathetic voice.

Kokila looked at Rajneesh and nodded her head in silence as she was saying, 'Prodigal man come. Our child needs you.'

Adhunika shouted again, 'Papa! Please come back. I do not need farmhouse I need you.'

Rajneesh rushed and planted a kiss on Adhunika's forehead.

The Last Ride Together

Ever since Deepika had walked out of my world — black and grey world and some time blazing with fire at heart, I had been suffering from plethora of mental pain by her memories — sweet and sour memory. The more I tried to forget her more she clung to my mind. I became habitual to bear all sorts of adversities and had learnt to live with destitution. It went on for years together — for about twenty five years. We had lived together for a short time and were getting married very shortly. It was she who had entered my bohemian world of her own and I was very happy to have her. Naturally, I loved her and understood the meaning of life after my living in together with her.

Before she came to live with me, I was living in bad faith; what I desired I denied it, what I was; I denied it to every woman that came in my contact. For my physical need, there were many call girls. I chose some of them for my sexual need. I had many facets. You might call me eccentric, to some extent I was, but I was sensible and conscious of my wallet. I always spent only twenty percent of my income on these call girls. There was no emotional attachment with them. You might think I was not an emotional being. It was not so, I was super-fully emotional, but not with these flesh vendors. They were like any commodity of daily use such as newspaper, or telephone. Visiting them was like going to the green grocers or going to cinema hall, but not like purchase of canvases, paints and brushes. This was totally a different phenomenon. It was an investment on my creative pursuit. Now you might have understood that in spite of being an eccentric man, I was a normal being like any other citizen of the town.

As I had many facets, I was a good son to my mother; I regarded her as an ideal mother. She protected all who came in her fold like her own children. She did not go to temple or to saints or on pilgrimage to religious places, but she cared for the have-nots and shared their sorrows. She medicated those, who could not afford the fee of *angrezi* doctors.

When I left home, she said, 'Krishna never hurt the *gopies,* never play with their sentiments.' And inspite of my fooling around with young lasses, I never played with the honour and respect of women. Naturally I wanted to prove to be a good man. Of course I ogled them, but I denied to my normal self. Wasn't it living in bad faith? Of course, it was bad faith.

But as a teacher, I lived in good faith. I tried to do my best to impart the best possible knowledge. Students called me good teacher, which I was or not I could never know. All this I did just to prove that I was better than other teachers. I was in a rat race. I was always in search of admiration. But fortunately or unfortunately, this did not bring back my love, my sweet heart, my Deepika who deserted me, when I needed her terribly

My colleagues called me a fool — a donkey.

'What was the government paying to teachers? Peanuts? So why should we bother for students,' my colleagues often grumbled. They laughed at me and commented that I was the most selfish man. I work hard for name for admiration. In the evening I would think of my colleague's comments on me. I introspected for hours together. Yes, I was selfish; I wanted to be admired by the beautiful young girls. It was a kind of imaginative sex satisfaction. My colleagues were more honest about themselves than I was to my self. They did what they believed. I did what was expected of a teacher. But such moments of introspection and engrossment in self evaluation gave me some temporary freedom from the disease of separation from Deepika. Another way of forgetting her was to plunge in the creative trip or listening to music. The *gazals* would lighten my agony, pain of separation from Deepika. Smoking and drinking added joy to relish the love's agony.

All my girl friends knew that Deepika had left me for good. They often visited me to console me in one way or the other, but they never told me that Deepika will never come back to me. But I could not accept the fact that Deepika had deserted me. Pinky was among the most frequent visitors to my studio. 'Why are you ruining your life for a woman who deserted you for no rhyme and reason?' she advised me time and again.

'How does it matter to you?'

'Because, I am your well wisher and I can not see you in such agonized state of mind.'

'Pinky thanks for your sympathy. But I should not suspend my hopes and aspiration for Deepika to return.'

'Suppose she does not return, then?'

'How do you say so?'

'It is just supposition.'

I had no answer to her questions. But I kept up my vow to Deepika that I will share my life with her even after death. There were many more aspirants to settle with me, but to everyone, it was no with big N.

One thing I could never understand was that I never got angry at Deepika nor I cursed her. I had read and heard that the jilted lovers sometime become very revengeful and often try to harm their beloved. But in me such feelings never developed. I always thought of her welfare and happiness. I prayed every night before jumping on my empty bed that where ever she was she must be delectated. Such expression gave me the feeling of nearness to her in my imagination.

A few months and a year, I spent in her association, were full of delight and joy. She had brought a big change in my life. I centered my thoughts on her. And she was the inspiration for my all actions. I did not believe in God but I found a new God – 'Love is God' with capital G. Now when I had become centric, my friends called me super-fully eccentric; but I did not care for their comments. Only regret was that Deepika had gone out of my life. We had vowed to stand with each other and would not part even in death. One day she went to see her parents, with the promise that she would return after a week, but she never returned. I tried hard to meet her but all my efforts were futile.

For a few weeks I thought that she would turn up, but when she did not come back, I got panicky and all sorts of wild imagination disturbed me. 'Has she been fallen in bad hands? Has she been kidnapped for money? Has she met an accident?' Such thoughts were nightmare and were very frightening. So with the hope that she would be safe and sound, I decided to go and see her at her parent's house. One fine morning I took a flight for Jalpore and reached 777- Krishana Kunj. I ringed the doorbell. A young girl came out. 'Whom do you want to see?' she asked.

'Young lady my name is Krishna and I want to meet Deepika — a young woman who has come to live here. Please tell her that Krishna has come.'

She made me to sit on settee, went inside a pantry, and brought some cold drink and gave me a glass to drink.

'You wanted to see Deepika. Yes she was living here but she had gone away to see our ailing father; I am her elder sister Jutika.'

'Thank to my star she is alright.'

'What do you mean?'

'Since I had no news about her, so all these weeks I had been imagining all horrible things such as she might be kidnapped or fallen in the hands of bad elements or might have met with an accident. It was natural as I love her more than I love myself.'

'She is perfectly all right. As and when she comes I will tell her about your visit.'

I regretted that I could not meet her, but I had relief in mind that she was alright and one day she would join me again.

Time went on moving, the lovelorn pain decreased, but my love life stuck at Deepika. Only thing that I had to my credit, I went deeper and deeper in my creative pursuit. I travelled round the country, went through the Himalaya carrying the imagination of my beloved in my heart. Sometimes I imagined as if she was drenched in water in the waterfall and her sari was clinging to her body exposing her waxy and glossy skin which I treated in some of my oils. Some times she would rise in the tumult of the flooded subtle river and protested why I was looking at a nude in the waterfall. Her apparition would appear in the woods behind the tall deodar trees as if she was inviting me to make love with her in nature in aloofness on the bed of wild flowers. In the planes, during my expedition in Thar Desert, she would fetch water from the oasis and pour in my thirsty mouth. Or in town I would imagine as she is looming out of my abstracts. Such imagination kept me alive.

I always hoped that one day she would come back. But when I failed in my search for Deepika, I decided to leave the country and went away to Europe. I tried hard to find a substitute for Deepika. I kept myself busy with some work or the other. Writing, painting, meeting people, all consumed my time. Over-busy schedules lessened my lovelorn pain, but I could not throw out Deepika from mind. Life was taking many turns and twist mostly for pleasant spasms. But whenever I was alone at seashore, the image of Deepika would rise from deeper memory where it had been pushed by the new environment. The recollection of her image was not in the least agonized as it used to be a few months ago in India, but it was very inspiring for returning to my native land. I would feel as if she is on the deck of a ship and shouting behind the roaring waves that she has come to take me back to her fold. A broad grin would appear on my face. 'What a phenomenon is this love!' I would speak to myself. I visited Museums, Galleries, Monuments and churches in the company of her memories. Readers, you might think that I was mad, but I was not. It might be happening to all those experience the extremism of love for a woman. But in others' presence I would not show my feelings. I had a very strong will power to keep my secrets to my self and not to give any clue that I was a lovelorn man, otherwise they would make fun of me, and they would laugh at me.

'In fact, man in modern age is so different — especially in the western world, that they are no more than robots. They have brain but no feelings just as you put petrol in your car and you can drive it, you push dollars in a man's hand he will act for you as you want. I am not fanatic nor I am against modernity, but certainly I may say that men without feelings are like computers. They care little for their Deepikas.

I wrote a series of letters to Deepika, but she did not respond a single one. Last one I wrote to Jutika, Deepika's friend. 'Dear Jutika, I wrote dozens of letters to Deepika, but she did not reply a single one. I am thousands miles away in a country known as Cape with Heaven. But my heaven is when Deepika is with me. I wonder what wrong I have done to her that she refuses even to communicate with me. Either my letters are not delivered to her or she is being forced not to write to me. I used the word forced with a presumption that we both had an understanding to live life together; and I have no cause to believe that she has changed her mind. I really want to know the reality. Please write to me back even if it is against hopes of my hope – in the sense that Deepika wants to settle with some one else. If I do not hear from you, I would have no alternative except coming back to India and to find out the real facts.'

Days, weeks and a month passed I did not receive any reply. But by then I got involved seriously in creative work, for an exhibition in a gallery at walking street. The desire to communicate with Deepika diminished to zero degree. But it was a passing phase. I made several girl friends. They thronged my makeshift studio at Montergade. Inge Thompson often came and helped me in getting paintings photographed, getting the brochures published for the exhibition etc. One evening after getting drunk, she dragged me on the floor and tried to seduce me. I did not resist, but at the last moment, Deepika's image crept in mind, so I zipped my togs and got up. Inge was angry but when I related the story of Deepika, she laughed at me, 'You are an idiot. Think of the present. Why do you bother of the past?'

So, soon after the exhibition, I decided to fly back and made last efforts to meet Deepika for living in 'my present'. And one fine morning I was in Jalpore.

Jutika was not there, but I met her cousin, who told me that Deepika was in Delhi and married and mother of a girl child. For a moment I was stunned, but I retrieved my composure and said that I wish I could adopt her daughter as my daughter. He replied that it was too small and she would not be able to live without her mother. I was silent. I was carrying some toffees in my bag so I took out the packet and distributed among their children. At least I got the factual information regarding my love; then onward I never tried to meet her, as I realized that it would be bad if I disturbed her married life.

I had left my position as professor at the university long back. And soon after returning from Europe, I left Chandpore and built a Garden cottage, where I could stay and carry out my creative pursuit. My relationship and later on parting away with Deepika, affected not only me but my mother also. She was terribly unhappy, about my situation. She often asked me to take her to Deepika's house so that she might talk to her parents, but I told her that she should stay away from my problems. Besides now nothing could be done as she was married.

Time passed on. One thing I was sure of that she would not return to me. Now I did not feel the lovelorn pain. I was totally a different person — a silent, sober and grim man. Of course I did not cease to love my own self I reorganized myself. After my creative pursuit I devoted my time for the welfare of girl-children. I never talked about her to anyone. Though, I could not push her out of mind, but I stopped thinking of her. Naturally she was a wife of some other man then. Many friends advised me of getting settled with some one or the other and several girls were eyeing on me. But I resolved not to have another chance. Besides

I would not be honest about my feelings to the new entrants as I had consumed those kinds of entire feelings and emotions for Deepika. For that matter I was quite blank and I wanted to maintain this blankness for many reasons. One reason was to sublimate my feelings for creative pursuit. And to a considerable extent I achieved some success. It gave my soul some satisfaction. For socializing I had many girl friends, but when any one insisted to the point of getting settled, I stopped visiting her or inviting her. In such course of action I lost many of them, but it did not affect me in any way. I had learnt to live a life of loner in self love.

One of the main problems that I faced then was finance. My running after Deepika and long distance travelling consumed my bank balance. The monthly pay packet had stopped long ago before my tour to Europe as I left the university. I lost the contacts of my art connoisseurs who often bought my paintings. Some of them – specially the American had left the country due to strained relations between India and America. I could not expect any assistance from my parents; rather they expected some assistance from me as they were aging. My friends showed their back and refused any kind of help. The gallery keepers who often ran after me to trade on my paintings refused to entertain me to buy my paintings. But luckily I had enough paintings to keep them in some new art gallery on consignment basis. Besides, I made a trip to Bombay and went to my permanent art connoisseurs who owed me some money. I collected the payments and kept new paintings with them for sale consideration. It took me a year's time to have breathing conditions. I painted some new canvasses and exhibited in Delhi and Bombay. Again I was rolling in the market. During this bleak period many gallery keepers cheated me and neither returned the paintings nor paid for them. I had no alternative except to bear the losses.

The subject of my paintings changed. I searched new areas of my creative pursuit, the personal love changed into universal love. Cutting off from Deepika did not diminish my emotion of love, rather it grew in abundance. I loved birds, animals, flora and fauna. Above all I loved women, not amorously, but sublimely. Child especially girl child took my special attention. People thought that I was a saint, but I claimed to be a human being only, as I still had all those weaknesses which a common man had. For my sexual need I still went to female sex vendors. It was necessary for my mental health. But there was change in my attitude towards them. Earlier I treated them like any commodity of daily use but now I had some feelings for them also I experienced the blending of orgiastic feeling with loving feeling. I realized that they were also human beings. Only difference was that their profession was looked down upon by and large. I found that except a few, they were not unscrupulous women. They too had some ethics, which they followed strictly.

When ever I met the old common friends in parties or in small gatherings, who knew Deepika, they often asked me if I was in touch with her. I often kept quiet. And my silence conveyed every thing to them. On one of such occasions, Tarun — one close friend told me that he had met Deepika in a festival; she had grown gray haired and looked older for her age. I did not express my feelings, nor did I want to get into old conditions. Only thing I said was that I too had grown white hair, but certainly I will never grow old.

When I met Deepika for the first time, she was much younger than me. In term of years the difference was of 16 years, but mentally and virility I was younger than her. And even till late my agility, my stamina and my mind functioned like a young man of 36. I wonder what went wrong with Deepika as Tarun said that she looked old. All this, I thought in mind, but did not express to my friends.

After wandering around in the country and abroad I had established my self again with reasonable success and built a small estate and lived on it. I had come across some new friends who were very sympathetic to me and wanted me to settle with some girl or the other, but I refused to accept such suggestions. I had stopped drinking, and smoking. I was living with austerity. I had created a new world and practically I had forgotten Deepika.

I was recouping my old humour and carefree ways of living. I had cut off from all old girl friends and had made some new ones and a new aura was developing around me, when some thing happened.

It was August 22, 2001 — a sunny day and after a brief shower last night, the trees were looking fresh. The squirrels were frisking around on the lush green lawn. A dove was cooing in the neem tree and a cuckoo was singing melodiously in the river side mango tree. The nature was in its best attire; and while I was sitting in the living room watching its beauty, the telephone rang.

'Hello this is Krishna from art studio.'

'Guess who is speaking?'

'Sorry I could not recognise your voice'

'Some one from your old College.'

'Except one girl I am not in touch with any one for the last three decade.'

'Whom did you call your life?'

'Deepika! What a pleasant surprise. You are Deepika.'

'Yes, I am Deepika.'

'Where are you speaking from?'

'From Gurgaon.'

'I am in Gurgaon. I can come to pick you up tell me where are you in Gurgaon.'

'I am in U. Vihar. It is a place Near American Express.'

'It is not more than ten minutes walking distance from my place.'

'I'm coming to see you. Please tell me the name of your company.'

After 29 years of interval I heard her voice.

She gave me her telephone number. and her company's name. She told me that she would be going home, but she would meet me next day. It was very exciting to hear Deepika's voice after long 29 years. After a long time, I was feeling ecstatic. I thanked my stars. It looked that every thing was vibrating with delectation. Though, I knew that it would be meeting her as an old friend and not as my beloved as she had a family of her own, but it did not affect my delight in the least.

Next day Deepika telephoned me and told me that she would be busy for few days, but she would come to see me. On Tuesday 28 August she telephoned.

'My driver is on leave and I do not know how to go back to my home. If any of my friends is going to Delhi, please ask him to give me lift.'

'Deepika, why do you worry? I will reach you to your home in my old Fiat. Incidentally you wanted to visit me but you did not come. I was eagerly waiting for you visit.'

'I was busy in the office and at home with some domestic problems, so I could not make it. But One day I will visit your studio.'

'It is alright. In fact I was anxious to see you. So we shall be meeting in the evening soon after your office is closed.'

Deepika was working in Hudson Brampton and Associates for the last three years. But either of us did not know about each other's existence at a walking distance. But one thing I was sure that some common friend had been in touch with her otherwise how she could get my telephone number. All the same it did not matter who gave her my telephone contact or how did she have it. I was simply delighted that we had established communication. And this evening I would be seeing her after a long interval of 29 years.

I got ready much before the appointed time and looked every now and then on hmt sona at my wrist. I had already cleaned my sweet heart fiat and it was ready for drive.

It was seven minutes to Five o'clock when I steered the car, and reached there right in time. After parking the car in the parking arena, I went to the reception and asked for Deepika. The receptionist telephoned her that I was waiting for her. The receptionist told me that she was just coming. She did not take more than half a minute. The door of the lift opened and she walked out. I did not make any mistake in recognizing her and I clamped her in my arms. We walked out of the office to the parking arena.

I opened the front door for her and once she was seated I closed the door and sat on the wheel. I drove out and came on the road. Once I was out of the crowd, the first thing I asked her was that how she recognised me in such appearance. She had seen me in very fashionable dress with French cut beard and now I was in Kurta and Nehru pajama with long beard and long curls falling on the shoulders. She said that she had seen me many times on the TV. – especially when I was in Kargil during Pakistani aggression in 1999. I told her that there was so much to tell her, and I did not know where to begin with.

I looked at her and asked her, 'What happened to your long hair?'

'Long time back before I was married off. I had gone to Trienniale exhibition: and while I was going home after seeing the exhibition in a bus, some one cut my hair, which I realized when I alighted from the bus.'

'How come you got married, when you had resolved that either you will marry me or will not marry any one at all?'

'My grand father exploited me emotionally. While he was ailing he asked me that his soul will not rest in peace after the death, if I do not marry this young man – – means my husband. So I had no way out except to accept his insistence.'

I did not want to embarrass her by saying that I did not break my vow. Naturally I still cared so much for her that I did not want to see her slightest unhappy. So after a momentary pause I said, 'I had been searching for you and visited your father's house in Krishana Kunj. Your cousin told me that you were married.'

'That is not my father's house. That is a house of our far off relatives'

'All right, Deepika, tell me are you happy in life.'

She looked at me and said, 'I have adjusted well in life, and doing my duty as any normal woman does.'

While we were exchanging notes about our past, we reached her house. Her house was not a very big one and it was not whitewashed for long time it looked very droopy and grey, but it was neatly set. She introduced me to her daughter, who was a beautiful child. She treated me with a cup of tea and after half an hour, Deepika hinted that she had to visit some friend's house which implied that I should leave them. So I left her place.

My curiosity to see her was over. Now she was like any one else as a friend to me. But in deeper memory she was still my love. What though she was not with me. After a few days, I invited her for tea. She did accept my invitation and visited my studio with one of her colleague. For a few months we kept in touch with each other. On her birthday on 18 October, I visited her in her office and presented her fresh flowers as a token of good wishes. That was my last visit to her.

After a few days of her birthday I telephoned her. She said, 'Krish when I talk to you some thing happens to me. I feel sad and feel bad for myself and such feelings linger on for days together, so please it is better that I should not telephone.'

'Deepika, it is perfectly alright. I hate to see you unhappy or sad.'

That was the last conversation I had, Whatever might had happened to me, I consoled myself at least I loved a girl with my heart and soul. She too loved me. What though if she is not with me, at least her memories are alive in my heart?

Whenever I drive my darling maruti and hear the gazals by Jagjit and Chitra Singh, it reminds me of my sweet heart fiat and Last Ride Together with Deepika.